BLACK BLUEGRASS

12 SHORT STORIES

NO SWEAT

Black Bluegrass

No Sweat
Copyright © 2018 No Sweat
Published By
2018 OLD SEVENTY CREEK FIRST EDITION

Published in the United States by:
Old Seventy Creel Press
Rudy Thomas, Editor & Publisher
P. O. Box 204
Albany, Kentucky 42602
This work published herein is fiction. Any Similarity to individuals, past or present,
is not intended and purely coincidental.

ISBN: 0-99823743-4
ISBN-13: **978-0-9982374-3-5**

A good book is a sandcastle no wave can destroy.
No sweat

DEDICATION

My existence as an author would be nothing if not for my precious wife, Chesteen, my guiding light, Lindy Yeager, my writing mentor, Guy Davenport and my true friend and editor, Rudy Thomas.

Besides them, I would also like to dedicate this book to my mother, Nancy Lou McClanahan, my grandfather, "Daddy-Mack" McClanahan, my grandmother, Freda Peters, my daughter, Nancy Robbins and my two grandsons, Lance and Barrett.

I must also mention my dedicated teachers who did so much to help mold me and have proven golden throughout my life among them, especially those, going out of their way to steer me in the right direction; my Irvine Graded school fourth-grade teacher, Mrs. Laura Tuttle; my Irvine High School Latin and Journalism teacher, Mrs. Leslie Jones; my beleaguered Irvine High School principal, Joe Ohr; my Troop 144 Boy Scout Master, Charles Vanhuss; my Eastern Kentucky University English professor, Charles Whitaker; and my Eastern Kentucky University swim coach, Donald Combs.

And last, my old comrades in many memorable adventures, Charles Chappell, Larry Lynch, Bo Bennett, Jeff Schmidt, Wallace Scott "Doc" Lewis, Howard Farris, Eddie Woolery, Richard Cackling, Charles Harris, Gary Stone, Jim Isselhardt, John McQuithy, Robert Masters, Ken Bellamy and Alan Jones.

Table of Contents

How the title relates to these stories

"Black bluegrass is a resistant species of grass found only in one region in the world, eastern Kentucky. It is an ancient grass, believed, at one time, to have been fed upon by dinosaurs and early man. It's earliest origins have been discovered in a remote area on Barnes Mountain in Estill County, behind a hog lot and a chicken coop full of black roosters, along a ridge of crunchy soil composed in part of coal, slate and black agate; a place deep in the woods, where crows, buzzards and starlings are seen roosting in massive flocks. Over millions of years, as Black Bluegrass began to spread toward Lexington, it came out of the black woods and was bleached by the open air and light, oddly turning it to a certain hue of blueness, a true, wildcat blue depending on the angle of the sun's crepuscular rays. When Daniel Boone first floundered into Kentucky wearing his coonskin hat and clinging to "Old Betsy," he set up camp just outside of Lexington and saw the unique grass and after much deliberation, named it: "Blue Grass," never knowing its true origin."

NO SWEAT

1. Me and Daisy

I felt a certain calm as I took in the Kentucky River's musk and jade soul. The buzzards were just starting to take to the sky. I had grown up on the Kentucky River and my return to her made me feel like a Saturday morning boy all over again. I was the first on this day to go across the Valley View Ferry, the oldest in Kentucky. The man running it didn't speak and that was fine, I needed the solitude.

When the ferry made it over, I got back in my car and drove following the complicated directions I had been given, making many turns through the mountains with each turn taking me farther away from civilization. After I found myself on a narrow and tree-canopied road which kept meandering downward along a cliff, I came to my end. In front of me, in the cool and darksome deep hollow, in all its pristine Appalachian glory, was Marble Creek; everything it must have been like since the dawn of time. Off to my left, going upward, I noticed a rough road. I followed it past an abandoned school bus. As I looked up, I spotted a large house built out and over a cut in a cliff. I admired the rockwork which had gone into the construction for the foundation of the house and knew as I began stepping onto a laid stone staircase going up the mountain that someone had gone to great lengths to carve out a place in this wilderness.

Soon, I was greeted by a man in his fifties and his younger wife. I drank coffee with them and listened to his unquestionable belief that the hollow had once been a refuge for nefarious beings. It was because of the handful of items he had shown me a few days earlier, which he had found while digging out for a pond, that intrigued me to come. From his house, we took his truck and he drove me further up into the hollow before letting me out. He then said, he had to go and drove off back down. I never saw him again until long after dark.

I've been a quasi-archeologist-digger for almost fifty years. Sometimes, a certain place will talk to you, especially when you are alone. It's a queer thing. I've had it happen more than once. It may be a gift. It certainly isn't superstition. You get a "special feel" at that place. You can all but see and sense the people who were once there; this clay-cut in the middle of nowhere was whispering to me and no sooner did I turn on my metal detector than it began sounding. Everywhere I turned I got another beep. I knelt in the sun as the temperature was already a killer and began digging with my army shovel. Everywhere, I dug I found relics; they were on top of the ground and just below. Sometimes, there was scattered charcoal and sometimes not. For the next twelve hours, I only paused from digging to drink the water which I had brought.

PART 2
When I walked to my car that was parked next to the house, I was greeted once again by the man who lived there. He asked if I had fun. I answered, yes, and

that I would be making several more trips up and down the mountain through the night before I was through. I was already fighting off leg cramps and was glad he had a cold beer waiting for me. I had dug so many relics that day and I knew it would take me several hours to get them to the car. After making six trips with filled packs and five-gallon buckets, I opted to quit, leaving at least two more trips worth of artifacts piled around an old stump.

It was at least midnight and the evening air had settled to a smoothing massage when the man asked me to come on back in. His cabin was spacious and the restfulness I found as we sipped moonshine sent my spirit akin to the near full moon which was casting a silver glaze over the shadows of the night.

The man was just finishing a wonderful story as to why he had been declared crazy and been able to dodge the Viet Nam War when abruptly, down over the cliff in the darkness below, we saw two pickups pull up to the creek and turn off their lights. At once, the man's eyes widened and before another word was spoken, he darted across the room and came running back while loading and pumping shotgun shells into the belly of his sawed-off Winchester 97; five shells went into her as he fled out the back door.

The woods had been so gloriously still but now they were alive as my newfound friend cut loose with curse words which even I had never heard -- and my father had been in the merchant marines during World War Two. No sooner did the saucy expletives echo throughout the region than did blasts erupt from his shotgun. And then, as the fifth shot was fired, cursing thundered from the other direction, and with it, rifle and pistol fire. Bullets began zinging upwards through the hollow and by the house.

My friend ran back into the house which now had evolved into something of a garrison, sweating with a territorial wildness of early man. He burst open a box of high-powered shotgun shells, reloaded, grabbed a handful, stuffing them in his pocket and then took a lever action Marlin 44 off the wall as he hurried back outside. Three shots hit the side of the house, one coming through a large open window, and that's when I suggested to his wife, in the calmest of manner which I could maintain, perhaps, it might be prudent to consider our turning off the lights. I had seen enough Westerns in my grandfather's theatre to know, we were sitting targets. Displaying very little urgency, the lady waited a few minutes and then obliged.

Several more bullets whizzed by the house, one hitting very close to the wall where I was crouched. I then I decided to sink another degree lower, crawling to a better protected area behind their stone fireplace. In close attendance with me was Daisy, the affable beagle which belonged to the newfound friend of mine and the alert and intelligent small dog which had been my companion throughout my dig. Daisy got up next to me wanting to play, having observed my crawling on the floor. I felt a little ashamed, as I held her snug against my body, a shield. If a bullet somehow ricocheted through the house and found us, it was Daisy, inevitably, that would likely be wounded. Her tail continued to wag as though it were the baton in the hand of a symphony conductor orchestrating George Gershwin's, AN AMERICAN IN PARIS.

PART 3

I have not had any formal combat training, but I had been raised in Estill County, Kentucky. I had jumped off the Irvine Bridge more times than anyone would believe and with my 55th birthday just 18 days away, I was beginning to appreciate how lucky I had been up until this point. Daisy was licking my face when I voiced to the man's wife, our force, as it were, was running out of shells, and, if my count to the sound differentiations was correct, I highly recommended, we should make some attempt to call in back up. As much as I regretted it, this meant the police, calling that the law broke all the codes in the mountains.

About 20 minutes passed with sporadic gunfire, and with Daisy and me all but married to each other, the police appeared in the hollow, three squad cars and one detective car fitted with blue lights and search lights. One brilliant search light shined through our front window, possessing the sun itself. For a moment, our fort became strangely-inanimate and silvery. As I scanned our confines, I could see a sly locked-smile on Daisy's face, letting me know she had been Pocahontas, and I, Captain John Smith. Normally, I go for ladies with dancing green eyes, but Daisy's dark-brown eyes had an alluring Raquel Welch intrigue and there was a jet-black rim around them as if she wore make-up. She looked straight at me with those mesmerizing eyes as if to say, she had no other friend in the world; to her, I was a 150-pound rabbit.

PART 4

For quite some time the police remained, never once venturing up to the house. I was thankful. I wasn't sure if I could explain my status in this situation and make it believable. Only Daisy could verify my statements. Being a full-blooded Estill Countian, I doubted, the police would believe that I was a great archeologist out to improve man's mind.

Daisy continued to stand on her hind legs, looking out the big window, defiant and happy all in bundle. She possessed almost orange-colored, floppy ears, and during the melee, I had found them to be wonderful covers while placing them over my eyes during silent prayer.

The police eventually re-stored quietness to the hollow. Daisy and me, faces side by side, gazed out the front window, seeing figures getting in their trucks. The two pickups went back up the road with the three cruisers and the detective's car following close behind.

I felt elated. Some victories go unnoticed. I looked over at Daisy, her tail was still wagging. Somehow, she understood. Dogs know more than we do, which ain't much.

PART 5

When my combatant friend returned from the battle, he laid his armament on an oak table and expressed dissatisfaction with the police having not arrested the trespassers. The very audacity of those drunks violating the tranquility of his hollow. Oh well, he resigned, as Daisy jumped up in my lap, we shouldn't let a little thing like this interrupt our drinking. After all, I had just discovered another Machu Picchu and survived the Alamo all in one night.

The man's wife looked across the table as he slid the quart of his second run-off rye, relaying, this kind of stuff went on all the time, usually about every month or so. I took another big drink from the quart jar and then gasped for air as my innards transformed into hell's worst flames. As the flames subsided, I theorized, it probably all had something to do with the fullness of the moon, though I doubted any anthropologist would ever venture into this hollow to conduct such studies.

"You know, of course," voiced my friend, "You'll never get out of here by taking the ferry. It shuts down after eight. You'll have to take the back roads to work your way out. You must go three miles over toward this way," he explained, taking a drink and getting a pencil, drawing a map on a small piece of scrap paper. "Then, you'll need to go five miles back over this way," he continued, drawing a line on the paper which was grossly disproportionate to his three-mile line which he had just drawn. "Once you get to this place, you go to this place, right here, it's got three roads that
veer off different ways." He then got another piece of paper. We had no scotch tape but this second piece of paper was to serve as a continuation of his original map, that is, if I connected it to the other in an exact correct angle. "Don't take the first or last road," he told me. "Or you'll wind up in nowhere. If you take this second road, you'll come out okay. It'll eventually lead you into Jack's Creek Pike. You should be able to figure your way from there. If you turn left back in here or go right over in there, there ain't no telling where you'll wind up."

Holding these instructions over a candle's dim light in one hand and moonshine in my other, I paused to reflect upon my abilities to navigate under such adverse conditions: I had been in horrible storm 50 miles off the north end of the Bahamian chain in the middle of the night in a small boat with drunken comrades at the helm. I had been lost in Wind Cave for several hours before finding a recognizable chamber. I had even picked up a "pigeon friend" at The LaGuardia airport and made it back to White Plains, New York. It was a moment that I began to appreciate Edgar Allan Poe, that part about, pondering weak and weary.

PART 6

After another drink, or was it two, maybe three, possibly four, I worked up the nerve to leave. I almost missed the first step out the back door. If I had fallen from there, I'd still be falling. Daisy wanted to go home with me. Our heartbreaking departure was like that one memorable scene in the movie, Gone with the Wind. Only. I did give a damn. Daisy's lick across my mired face got some of the dirt out of my eyes. I was thankful, as I had been unable to wash due to their dug well, being dry. Maybe now, with any luck, I'd be able to see the road.

August 6th, 2006, was already upon me. My waning conscience declared, I ought to be home before daylight as my family might begin to wonder. I pondered, what would Howard Carter, Schliemann, or Luis Leaky do? All my Estill county instincts knew, a gauntlet of police most likely laid before me; it was one matter to evade the wilderness, survive a gun battle, another to escape civilization's blue lights.

I never gave the map one second of consideration, pitching it out the window over a cliff as I high-beamed through a surreal forest. The moonshine took a bad hold on me and before I knew it, I was on automatic control, almost like Christopher Columbus and Kit
Carson. I was guiding and "feeling" myself back via the earth's mysterious forces and mysterious even more--love, akin to a debauched homing pigeon. I could see a slight rise of lights on the horizon from time to time and I followed them as best the course allowed.

After more than an hour, I found myself on a side street coming up in the middle onto Main Street in a city named, Versailles. I didn't have the slightest notion which way to go and once more fell back on my moonshine instincts for guidance. The streets were as vacant as if someone in another county had been giving away government cheese. I was lucky for a few blocks and then I came to a four-way red light. At the light a local police cruiser pulled up at another angle; it was the longest of lights, and I supposed, inevitably, I was going to be reviewing the backside of some jail's door.

PART 7
Lindbergh managed to fly all through the night and avoid perils, but he never came to a stop light facing a Versailles policeman. If he had drunk the same moonshine which I had consumed, history would have been different. I just kept looking at the light, pretending, I was innocent, maybe headed to some place for work--even church. The color of that light was my only concern. The light turned green and I drove past the policeman with a steadiness of which Peter O'Toole owned in Lawrence of Arabia. Before dawn, I somehow stumbled home. Thomas, my cat, came up to me and fussed as I unloaded the car.

As the sun broke across the mountains, I sat in my front yard. I watched the newspaper being delivered while washing the relics which I had unloaded into an elongated pile, covering my entire front porch, a mound well over two-feet high, which ran for over twelve feet or more. There was everything from the time period of the late 1700's all the way up to the 1890's; most of the items were from the Civil War period.

The more I sat and looked at each piece, the more I realized, my newfound friend in the hollow had been correct in what he had first stated to me. Indeed, there had been nefariousness up in that hollow at one time. From all the relic evidence, it became apparent that I had discovered a Civil War cathouse; fancy yellow-ware chamber pots; delftware; cream-ware; black glass champagne and beer bottles; gold-gilded sash pins with one having the word: "HICKCOCK" on it; fancy pat. 1851 Goodyear rubber hairpins and buttons; one rubber item with the word "BAILY" scratched on its backside; decorative English blue and pink transfer ware and ironstone dishes; and two and three tine pewter dinnerware; syringes from the time when they were often used to treat venereal disease; small, pontiled medicine bottles; elaborate shoe heels; small iron shoe hooks for buttoning laces; tiny glass and porcelain beads and buttons of all colors and imagination; coffee grinders; silver coins from America and France; ornamental 1862 pat. lamps; showy cut glass bowls; decorated pipes with fancy stems; brass stirrups; a fancy stove with a big emblem on its front and the words: "E PLURIBUS UNION;" iron roller wheels for furniture and beds, one having a white porcelain wheel; gold rings; porcelain dolls. heads, arms and legs; fancy scissors; personalized thimbles; and so many relics that screamed this place was not average and that it was most likely inhabited by women as well as men.

Another assemblage of clues came from the Civil War relics. There were no musket Minnie's, only various round ball pistol bullets and brass rim- fired shell casings with the initials, "US" in the middle of them. There was one Springfield bayonet, but it had been converted into a candle holder. There were officer's buttons, a Kentucky button depicting our state symbol of two men shaking hands, buttons from Zouave uniforms and cuff buttons from the artillery and infantry. There was also a beautiful silvered button with a star in its middle possessing the word "BRAKEMAN" running along it edge, apparently, even the Civil War railroaders employed by the US government knew of the place. I found several officer sword parts and two nice pocket knives, one being a bone handled Barlow and the other, a solid brass knife owning a "U" at the top of it, an eagle with its wings outstretched in the middle, and a "S" below on the other end of the knife. Jew's harps, harmonica reeds, pontiled swirl marbles, small white, marble, square gaming pieces. There were so many relics and they all kept saying, this was a place where people relaxed and enjoyed themselves. The bones I found showed the people who had once live there preferred pork, but there was also beef, turkey, chicken and rabbit. Along with them, I found meat cleavers and various fireplace items, such as long- handled, cast steel two-tine forks and iron hooks for which to hang pots.

PART 8

It was fitting, someone from Estill County, Kentucky, discovering a whore house, but, generally, they are active. I continued thinking, about five or six miles off, as the crow flies, there was Camp Nelson; it had been a Civil War depot that had been the home to some 4,000 soldiers for over four years. Surely, there had to be some bored soldiers which thought of other things besides State's Rights, slavery and all that stuff. In every American war, there has always been that one soldier from Estill County, or other soldiers possessing an Estill County heart, who went AWOL or deserted. If these soldiers possessed knowledge regarding the location of a house of ill-repute, even if it was five or six miles as the crow flew, surely, they'd be the crows.

2. CAMP NELSON, KENTUCKY

Jessamine County, should be renamed Jesse James County. It's almost worse than Estill County. I would never have gone into that godforsaken region if not for the lure of all the Civil War relics which had been discarded by the thousands of soldiers throughout the length of the entire war. Camp Nelson was Abraham Lincoln's experimental Civil War city, a Union depot which maintained four thousand soldiers over an area covering four thousand acres; soldiers who had lived there never one day dreaming that I would be searching for their garbage.

When Ezekiel Jones and I were slithering around in camouflage, metal-detecting Camp Nelson as twilight approached, we rendezvoused in deep woods and began our trek back to our vehicle. Just as we topped the steep mountain we had climbed, we heard a stern voice sound directly at us. "HOLD IT RIGHT THERE!"

We both froze in our tracks.

The threatening voice was so close you could touch it, having grown up in Estill County, I knew those kind of voices; they were never good. My eyes scanned, seeing nothing but stark woods. I moved my head toward Zeke and noticed, he was taking an ever-so-low back step.

It was that very queer time of the day when images dissolve into a grey nothing, the apex of twilight. He's not leaving me here, holding the bag, I thought. Like all Estill Countians, I was allergic to the law. In an instant, I turned, taking one giant leap for mankind, or at least, one of its lower representatives; I became an Appalachian gazelle forgetting all about The Civil War, except for retreat.

PART 2
I was on my third leap when a rifle cracked loose and the tree which was inches from my face, exploded from its bullet. I then went into a full zigzag pattern. At a steady walk and in good condition, it took about twenty minutes to hike up the mountain which Zeke and I were on. I was at the bottom of it in less than in thirty seconds.

I paused in the darkness. Before me was the rush of a wild creek. I continued to pause, attempting to gather my wits and assess my situation. There was no time to ask questions. Someone crazy was after me. I looked upwards at the black mountain and could see, two lights heading down towards my direction. Who in the hell are those guys, I thought? I knew they would shoot and kill me if they got the chance, their blood was up. I didn't have time to think any farther. I headed downstream, running hard at first along the creek, guess-jumping every step, constantly thankful for not
falling and for any flat white rocks I spotted. I continued to run hard another three

hundred yards before I paused to get my breath. I was at a bend in the creek. The lights were still coming. Three, maybe four minutes away. I knew, if I continued to run like I was doing, I would soon collapse. My heart was pounding and my mouth was dry. Slow down, pace yourself, I said. You swam long-distance in college for Don Combs, you can beat these guys.

PART 3

It was late fall; the temperature was dropping fast. It was even colder along the creek, Hickman Creek, rushing with a force from the frigid rains it had received for several days prior to Zeke and me going metal detecting. The creek, and the 500-foot palisades which encompassed the area, the highest cliffs in Kentucky along the Kentucky River, were the natural boundaries, and why this area had been selected for the protection of Camp Nelson during the Civil War.

I paced for a solid half-hour with my pursuers holding at about their same distance; since they possessed lights and guns and possible knowledge of the area, I knew, they had all the advantages. And then it happened, my luck ran out; I had paced to a place where the mountain came up close next to the creek. My world had narrowed. I had to make a choice, whether to try and climb the mountain or attempt to cross the creek, which now, was more of a river than any creek.

I chose the water.

I had been swimming in creeks and on the Kentucky River soon after I had learned to walk. I grew up on the Kentucky River. And on this night, at this moment, water was my edge. Those pursuers could not know, when I was 20 years old, I was swimming long-distance for one of the best swim teams in America as the fastest native Kentuckian swimmer in the state. I chose the raging water, for I guessed, whoever was pursuing me, would not try to cross. They would never believe that anyone would try it either. I also contemplated if I attempted to climb that mountain, I would lose ground and they would surely spot me in my attempt.

It was a life or death choice.

The moment I stepped into the creek my leg went almost numb, the water was ice-cold. I went on. In a few steps, I was up to my chest. The force of the creek pushed hard against my legs and body, trying to grab me and wash me downstream. Each step was a challenge, a test unto me against nature and all I was; every step I took, I touched onto an uneven bottom, some more slippery than others. I knew, if I went down, I was dead. I'm not sure how I got my legs to move or my body to hold but resolve continued to own me. Stepping out onto the other side, I felt little relief; a clock was ticking inside my head. In seconds, my trackers would have me. I stepped a few steps more on rocky ground, wet,

15

frozen, exhausted. Then, I collapsed and crawled over the gravels to a solitary boulder which stood before me; I wrapped my body behind it.

The moment I was behind the rock, two bright lights shinned upon my boulder and all around. I could almost feel those lights; they were starving.

 I held still.

Seven shots rang out above the noise of the rushing water. All were shot in my direction, one hitting the gravels and the others going through the woods behind me.

PART 4
If they crossed, I was at their mercy. The lights continued to shine. Then, they stopped. I snake-eyed around from the base of my rock. The two lights were going up the black mountain on the other side.

I lay still.

Once the lights reached the top of the mountain, they shined back down through the woods in different directions. One light went along the crest of the ridge back towards where the chase had erupted; the other followed the ridge on downstream.
I didn't know where I was. Through it all, I had managed to keep my head and toboggan dry. That saved me. I decided to climb the mountain behind me. An Estill County boy knows when he has beat death, even but for the moment. I wasn't in any rush to re-cross the creek. If I could make it up to the mountain top, I would gain more distance from my pursuers and be able to get my bearings; it was cave-black in this hollow, and the night air filled with frost.

The mountain was steep.

I kept hugging the ground with my feet turned sideways while making the climb. It was the slowest climb up any mountain I had ever made. My metal detector was being used as a lifesaving grappling hook. When I got to the top of the mountain, parts of me had dried out from my body heat, but nothing was so dry as my mouth. I was very thirsty.

It felt wonderful to find a level place. Fortunately, I stepped into a small clearing; the cosmos seemed to smile and encompass me. A biting chill met my cheeks. I had never seen it this wondrous; the stars were so close.

I felt very alone.

Two mountains over, there were the distant lights to the entrance of Camp

Nelson. My heart sank. I was much farther away than I thought, farther downstream and a full mountain farther over. Behind me, there was nothing but a ghostly darkness. I was lost yet I held calm. I wondered, *is Zeke alive?*

Off to my left, miles away, lived an old man, named, Gerald. If I could make it to his log cabin, he would offer me refuge. Straight above in the sky, where I guessed Gerald's cabin could be, was the Big Dipper. The North Star lay just off it. If I could follow that star through the woods, I could find Gerald. I angled toward the star and stepped through tall weeds, heading down the mountain in a different direction from which I had earlier traveled. The weeds were frozen and crunched beneath my feet. I went back into the woods and the sky disappeared. Blackness was again upon me.

PART 5
I sensed, I was in a dark dream. I could see nothing. I was in black and going downward. I reached a point where the steepness became extreme.

I sat down and began sliding. I slid for a long way, all the while sensing something was not right. I came to a small tree wedged between my legs. My legs and feet went past the tree and stretched out over nothingness. I paused; there was a difference in the air, lighter, colder. My eyes kept adjusting to the darkness. In the blackest of black, I began to see. It was queer, a darkish dream, a nightmare. I saw, shadowy forms.

My heart stopped.

Before me, as a sheer drop, a good 300 feet. My feet were dangling over a cliff. All that was saving me was the tiny tree between my legs, a pitiful tree possibly an inch in diameter.

 Straight below, was the vast black hollow where the creek churned. To both sides of me were more cliffs. If I went over, it could be years before parts of my skeleton would ever be found, and likely, never. I brought my feet back in. Dug in my heels. Carefully, I began to scoot back upwards through the darkness, clinging to anything my hands and feet could find, finally coming to a place where I laid on my back and looked up into the night. I had survived death once more.

PART 6
I couldn't go back off to my right, my pursuers might still be there. So, I made a goodly hike to my left, trying to sense the mountain's geographical lay, before I attempted another descent. Eventually, I found myself back in the hollow and facing the creek. This time, hopefully, there was no one trying to kill me.

Why had those men been so determined to murder me? Had they lost a marijuana patch? Had someone stolen a cow or tractor from their farm? No common farmer would be so hell-bound to murder a stranger. It had to be marijuana, I thought.

As I entered once again into the creek, the pain from the icy water shot back. Two-thirds the way over, I almost fell. When I got across, I stood but a second. The temperature had to be zero if not below. To remain still was to freeze to death. I took a step and then another. A few minutes later, my heart sank. I could not believe it, I was facing the creek again. How could this be? And it was wider than ever.

How?

Somewhere upstream, I realized, Hickman Creek had forked. I was now in the middle of that fork. It took me a moment to understand. I wanted to cry but couldn't. Again, I entered the creek. When I emerged on the other side, I was all but done. I had a mountain yet to climb if my instincts were right. It was black. I could not see any stars.

I began walking and in a short while I found myself in a field of briars. I turned my body backwards into them, unable to see anything. I had no idea that I had walked into the largest briar patch on earth, one which extended more than half-way up the mountain. The more I went into the hell the more I knew I could not turn back. My face, ears and hands became pierced, cut and tortured. Several times, I continued bent over and attempted to walk backwards, pushing the briars away and off me. As I moved upward, I fell into their painful clutches.

PART 7
Coming out of the briars and into woods, I fell. The freedom from the thorns was divine. I raised myself up and continued walking. My legs began to cramp. On top of the mountain, I came to a place I recognized; joy consumed me. All my dead reckoning had turned out to be right. I couldn't have done it again, ever. I walked to a barb wire fence. I was too weak to climb it. I couldn't lift a leg. I laid down and crawled under.

Gerald's wasn't much farther, a half mile, I guessed.

When I at long last stepped up to Gerald's cabin, I began beating on his back door. His daughter looked out the window, but wouldn't let me in. "Gerald!" I cried. "Let me in! It's No Sweat!"

The door opened. I collapsed on the floor. Gerald's pot belly stove was going strong. I raised and he helped me to it. I lay on the floor close to the stove. "Please get me water," I begged. He brought me a large glass. I asked for another. After drinking it, I lay on my back, telling my story to his family. I had been within a minute of life not making it to his cabin; my body was drained.

Gerald called my wife. She called Zeke at his home. After the gunmen had gone my way, he had made good in his escape. In an hour, Zeke was at Gerald's. Daybreak was coming.

For several days my body remained incredibly sore. I could barely move. I never told my story. Who would have ever believed it?

3. Ali Babba And the Forty Thieves

It was a muggy night in Irvine, Kentucky.

Dirt was on the streets in Irvine, Kentucky.

Dirt was on everything in Irvine, Kentucky.

Accumulated for years in Irvine, Kentucky.

Irvine was suffocating.

No town so gray.

So still.

I was sixteen years old. Living where I had always lived. In an apartment at the end of The Irvine Bridge over top my grandfather's theater. I was a lookout in the crow's nest of Irvine.

In my apartment, mosquitoes and granddaddy-long legs played tag along the stained-ceilings. Roaches whiskered about, sometimes flying out our back door. Rats hid behind our refrigerator, lapping up spilled beer and raising families on our garbage; they loved country ham.

Whatever the weather was, so was the apartment.

That night was nothing but sweat. It had nothing to do with weather. He told that a thousand times. If the words didn't come out of his mouth, they came out of his fists. As my grandmother, Momma Mack, said of him: "He enjoys standing in his own sunshine."

On this night, I was happy that mom and dad were gone; they wouldn't be back for several days. Off, some plaice, Old Fitzgerald drunk. Tonight, I would not be wounded by dad's drunken fists.

Our apartment was a tunnel of dark rooms which absorbed all the filth and noise Irvine owned: The trains hauling coal. The trucks from the quarry. The boats on the river. The cursing from the pool room. And the sounds from my grandfather's theatre.

I was an expert on those movie noises. Only a weathering layer of brick separated me from reality.

When Daddy-Mack was playing THE TEN COMMANDMENTS, I knew the soundtrack and dialog. I could hear it loud and clear through the brick wall of our apartment. I could tell you in advance when Charleton Heston was going to part the sea. Every year, Daddy-Mack would play that movie and Charleton Heston would part that sea.

The true Irvineites did not want to escape from Irvine no more than did the rats want to leave the garbage behind our refrigerator. "Irvine was a good place to live." I heard that a million times.

That's what Irvine said.

Our apartment contained a few pieces of broken and odd furniture which helped to conceal the clay catacombs of mud daubers. It was a narrow, flat-tar-roofed apartment with tall, filmy, BB-cracked windows at both ends, sanctuary windows, allowing me to peer out and see the life of Irvine below.

In our apartment, we had wasp-nest in the corners, starlings nesting in the eves, and survivalist bullfrogs that sometime came out to sing; frogs that had gotten away from dad after a night of gigging and cleaning.

Looking out the back windows, I could see the mountains and the Kentucky River; the front windows; the Irvine Bridge; the Riverview Hotel and Main Street.

Our apartment was just another brick bulwark double-lining Main Street. Some were built at the turn-of-the-century; some, a generation later; each different, but only a little. It was as though the same drunk brick-layer had laid every brick in the town and every town fifty miles away.

Irvine was with the outside world by its steel bridge; long, lime-painted, arching. Cumbersome. High above the Kentucky River. Sixty feet. I'd jumped it many times. Whistling as I'd go down. Keeping my body straight. Keeping my arms and legs together. Pushing off the muddy and rocky bottom after hitting. Sycamores rose and touched her belly. She was a corroding bridge owning blank histories of pigeons having generated themselves in her dark nooks. Lost pigeons surviving there because of the wasted corn in the bottoms. A bridge protecting them from the fangs below and the talons above.

I needed that bridge.

Railroad tracks ran under her. Grimy. Oily. Spilt coal. Rotting opossums. Wasted spikes. Busted whiskey bottles. The Louisville and Nashville Railroad. The L & N. A track skirting Irvine, hauling black energy raped from the mountains to unthankful progress. Up from the river, and its bootlegging boat dock located under the bridge, past the cane-break and kudzu and briars, the painted glass insulators atop the telephone poles beneath the bridge told the bridge's story, her forgotten colors:

Silver. A real silver. Once drawing my best friend and me under her to pretend we were Spartans; we leaped across emerald sewer streams to save Irvine from the Persians. At the head of those streams on the river was "OLD JIM," cane poles set, cursing the turtles, dreaming of a giant catfish.

Publisher's note:

On the following page is a sketch of "OLD JIM" drawn by No Sweat's good friend.

In No Sweat's own words, it is: "A sketch by the late Wallace Scott "DOC" LEWIS of Irvine, Kentucky, depicting "OLD JIM" who used to fish under the Irvine Bridge, dreaming of the day he would catch a giant catfish."

Maroon. A dead maroon. I had stood under that maroon watching my friend be pulled from the river, his pale body swollen and rotting, pieces of him falling apart when lifted, a smell which I can never forget.

Blue. A drunk blue. Slopped on by the jail-released, town drunk; one of my friend's father, a father he was more ashamed of than I was of mine. A blue having dripped on many vehicles crossing her. A blue grown black with the soot.

Up a narrow staircase, thirty-three straight steps, put you into our bare-floored living room, the middle room of our apartment. A small couch, chair and table. A record player holding a stack of Billy Holiday. To the left was the kitchen. Daddy-Mack knocked out a wall in the kitchen so we would have room to eat. He built a permanent table in between the wall with a large board. When doing this, he added a small room he made from pine boards and built in with four windows. That end room had steps leading down the back where I kept my lost homing pigeons that I had caught off the bridge; they pecked at the exposed theater brick composed in part of charcoal for grit. At the bottom of those splintery steps I could go in any direction to be in the middle of town or in the woods.

To the right of the living room was my bedroom, a lair just big enough for my small bed. In the ceiling was a skylight which had been partially covered but leaked when it rained. Beyond my room was mom and dad's bedroom. Dark. I rarely went in there. When I did, I would lift their heavy window curtain and lay it over my back, peering through the venetian blinds out of the cracked window. Looking out, I could see straight across Main Street and the bridge. Near the end of the bridge, was the tallest building in town, The Riverview Hotel, four stories and square. Off below, and near it, was the newspaper office, The Estill County Herald; the editor spent almost every Saturday night in our apartment, drunk. On Sunday, he glorified in a hang-over drink consisting of a raw egg, Tabasco and Worchester sauce, a shake of pepper, a squeeze of lemon and four ounces of vodka.

Especially if it was free.

On up Main street, was a little off-street named after my grandfather, Mack Street. He had donated the land to the city hen my mother's family had been rich. Those had been the good old days I had heard of but never experienced. The next block had been destroyed to make a concrete block grocery store called, The Family Key. Once it had been the site of a stage coach station. Now, it was a reminder of my family's drunken failure; where, along with my own father, my mom's big-shot brothers squandered a fortune. Next was a poolroom. And on up the street, another of my grandfather's theaters. But this theater was closed, the bones of an old mammoth of another age where my grandfather used to have stage shows, featuring singing cowboys who owned horses performing tricks. On up, another poolroom, a jewelry store paid for through a fake robbery, a clothing store owned by a delicate man who once fell drunk off his seat while playing the organ in the Methodist Church, and then a Chevrolet dealership operated by a smiling glass-eye who would do anything for money. Mack Street looped around the businesses and their apartments above them and came back around to Main Street. The block beyond was a straight row of seven evenly-fronted homes. These domains were inhabited by proud citizens; proud of their dry county; proud of their golf course; proud of their mountains kissing the bluegrass and proud of Adolph Rupp's wildcats.

The houses stopped at an ivy-covered Methodist Church, my church where I had gone for thirteen years without missing a Sunday. On past the church, was the Estill County High School; the plain school for the "poor country kids." A quarter mile on out was Irvine High School, my school, the academic school for the "rich city kids." Thirty miles beyond was the city of Winchester. You could buy liquor over there. Richmond, Kentucky was closer. Only twenty miles. And since liquor was closer in Richmond, Irvine went that way, crossing the bridge. East to west. West to east. Sun setting. Sun rising. Life to death. Death to life. Hell, to heaven. Heaven to hell. Reality to dream. Dream to reality. Irvine was addicted to Richmond.

 Irvine couldn't think of anything but Richmond.

"Old Jim" fished for that giant catfish underneath the Irvine Bridge. But never took an eye off that bridge. Many an empty pint sailed off the bridge down his way. He dodged and cursed. It was one matter to be pulled into the deep by that whiskery Kentucky Moby Dick, another, to be brained from above, by someone going to or leaving church.

On my side of the street beginning from the bridge was a row of two-story buildings. A doctor and her family occupied those upstairs apartments. She was a benevolent and understanding lady, keeping Irvine's dark secrets and giving Irvine the drugs it demanded to look at itself. Below, was a tomato of a creature, a strange chiropractor akin to the Andy's Mayberry. And before you got to the poolroom and theater, there was a finance office where the figuring was done not so much with numbers as it was with Jim Beam.

Daddy-Mack's theater had evolved from a livery stable. It had a wedge-shaped, neon lit marquee which hung out over the sidewalk. To stand back and look at it was to envision both a ship and the Alamo. Past the theater was an auto parts store. And on the corner, another pool room. The next block was taken up by the courthouse, a square, cut-sandstone structure looking more like a mausoleum than a place where so-called justice was served. The liar's bench in front of it was always full of men whittling cedar. During the Civil War, John Hunt Morgan's Calvary invaded Irvine. Took over the courthouse and burned down it's jail. Besides experts on the Bible, Irvine's citizens were historians and genealogist. Everyone descended from Daniel Boone. And if not, someone nearly as noble. Across the street on out towards Winchester, was the corner drug store. The offspring from its owner were Irvine High's "golden eagle" athletes. On up was a furniture store owned by a friendly man who was quiet and pinched pennies, a gentleman who enjoyed a little drink from time to time in our apartment and owned a 12-gauge Browning automatic which only shot twice. Past him was a hardware store where conversation was as American as its baseball gloves and bikes. Next was the Post Office and funeral home. Then, the procession of opposite facing Main Street homes which ran clear out and beyond the Christian Church. Only the Methodist and Christians ruled Main Street. The other off-brand religions were scattered thick and located throughout the hills.

From season to season, I would stare at the familiar faces from the windows of my parent's bedroom. No sight entertained me as much as did the sparrows. In the gray skies I would see the swifts dropping into the chimneys where they clung to life in their dark confines.

So, did Irvine.

The winter before that summer, Irvine strung multi-colored Christmas lights across its streets.

But it was still Irvine.

Irvine was like those lights, only a few worked.

That summer night was after the Tet Offensive, the opening of Planet of The Apes, Steppenwolf's BORN TO BE WILD and Martin Luther King's murder. Irvine heard about the Vietcong sneaking out of the jungle bushwhacking our soldiers. The Planet of The Apes packed the theater. Steppenwolf blared from every '55 Chevy and '63 corvette. Martin Luther King's death was, so what.

Irvine could have cared less.

One less black person.

One less ape.

Martin Luther King being the youngest man to ever win The Nobel Peace Prize, meant nothing. When Irvine High played Dunbar, a black school in Lexington, Irvine cheered: CHOCOLATE CAKE, CHOCOLATE PIE, DUNBAR, DUNBAR, DUMBAR HIGH!" There had been riots in over a hundred cities after the after-Martin Luther's assassination.
Fire bombs in Seattle. Mayor Daley ordered the Chicago police, shoot to kill.

During this period, I had been watching old French Foreign Legion movies on television. Gary Cooper and Ray Milland in BEAU GESTE; Victor Mature and Yvonne De Carlo in TIMBUKTU; Burt Lancaster in TEN TALL MEN; Ronald

Coleman in FOUR FEATHERS, and Gary Cooper and Douglas Fairbanks, Jr. in GUNGA DIN. Daddy-Mack's grandfather, Russell Bishop, had been a bugler in John Hunt Morgan's confederate Calvary. He had given Morgan his farm full of the finest thoroughbreds in the Bluegrass. When the war was over, "Bish" had lost everything. "Bish" hated Abraham Lincoln. He'd spit when Lincoln's name was mentioned. So, would Daddy-Mack. Daddy-Mack loved his grandfather. And I loved mine.

There was spit in me, too.

When Daddy-Mack built The Irvine Theater, he designed a queer, narrow, unlit, concrete, winding staircase like a concrete cobra. It led to an isolated spot above and behind the balcony, a small, cell-like room with two rows of four seats. And two metal pipe-like bars. When you sat down in one of the seats, your head almost scraped the ceiling. That dark pit was strictly for blacks. Irvine owned only a handful. They were poor and

"Knew their place."

On that hot summer night, Daddy-Mack didn't run the theater. He opened it but nobody but Herman Long, his old and faithful projectionist, showed up. Daddy-Mack locked the door and drove home. Herman went on up the street. I hung around out front looking for moths. I needed a Luna moth for my collection. Not finding any, I walked down the sidewalk to the end of the bridge, repeatedly throwing gravel up near a streetlight. The bats swooped in on the rocks thinking they were getting a meal. After a while I quit.

That's when I noticed commotion.

At the end of the bridge in the middle of the street, two large trucks were being parked. Four armed men kept getting in and out of them, directing each other until they were parked perfect to block traffic. Another ten or twelve armed men got out of the back of the trucks and walked up the street stopping in front of the theater. Some of them had on badges. The men passed boxes of shells to each other as they looked up and around at the tops of the buildings. I asked one of the men near the door of a truck what was going on?

"Get in the house, boy. Niggers!"

"What?"

"Ain-chu heard, son. Thousands of 'em. Headed here. Big bucks down from Detroit and Dayton, joined up with Richmond's. Freedom buses, gettin' revenge on that Martin Luther thing. Gonna burn Irvine. It's up to us to stop 'em. Now get a gun or get off the street!"

27

I hadn't heard anything about an attack. I watched as Irvine began to gather. In the next half hour, several hundred citizens. Bowie knives. Machetes. Pistols. Rifles. Shotguns. A Thompson machine gun. A fifty caliber Browning automatic. Grenades. A bazooka.

A bulldozer came down from Broadway onto Main Street and parked in between the two trucks placing its blade center in the street. The Irvine Bridge was secured.

Citizens began taking positions.

One man climbed up on top of the bridge. Several positioned themselves atop the Riverview Hotel. A young, bare chested deputy looked at me, pulling a stiletto from his boots. "We've got to hold this bridge," he ordered.

"I hope two boxes will be enough," spoke a man next to him, breaking down a double barrel.

"It'll have to be," answered the deputy. "There ain't no shell left in town."

Three men began pouring gasoline in empty Four Roses whiskey bottles and stuffing rags in the end making Molotov cocktails. "How do we get up there," one asked, looking at Daddy-Mack's marquee.

I walked the concerned citizens around back and showed them the exposed pipes and handholds near the gutters of one of the lower buildings. After we made it up on that roof, we walked upwards toward the theater's brick wall. I then showed them how to climb a certain brick chimney and then lean out over to the theater wall where part of one brick was gone. You had to lunge and make a good grab. It was hard. But I had done it many times.

No time in Irvine's history had been so important as this.

One by one we all made it, handing each other guns and bottles of gas. Once on top of the theater roof we walked to the front edge and scaled down the wall onto the marquee. The marquee had metal-like wall some three to four feet high which held neon lights and offered protection: a perfect spot looking down on whoever came across the bridge.

"I wanted buckshot but had to get fours," lamented an officer.

"Fours will be OK. Let 'em get in close. Shoot for the face," advised his companion."

I stayed for nearly an hour. It was black, balmy and silent. Usually, if you stood still long enough on the streets of Irvine late at night, you would see a cat or sometimes a fox. At least, a rat. But on this night, there was nothing. Sometimes a shell was heard being chambered. Someone kept coughing. You could see the lit ends of the cigarettes on top of The Riverview Hotel. Down at the river, a bullfrog periodically hollered. A whiskey bottle fell and broke. More defenders filtered in. Our force of concerned citizens had swollen to several hundred. I kept smelling gasoline while looking down and over at the bridge. The arches of it in the night reminded me of some giant praying mantis' arms arched and patiently waiting for death.

Then, all eyes focused on a runner coming down the street, hysterically shouting: "THE ATTACK IS COMING ON THE OTHER END OF TOWN! OUT OF WINCHESTER!" The runner, out of breath, collapsed in front of the theater. The citizens were upset, you could see in their faces and the way they jerked about in moving. They had been fooled! They had been told, and told flatly, that the busses were coming across the bridge. Headed hard down I-75, stopping in Richmond, and from there, they would come in at us off Highway 52.

Madness erupted.

Immediately, quasi-military posts were deserted; men jumped into the trucks at the end of the bridge and the bulldozer followed. Everyone except me and a few others remained. I climbed back down and went into our apartment. I got Dad's Colt Match Target Automatic 22 caliber pistol, Dad's favorite. And then I got our kitchen's biggest butcher knife. The one dad had stolen from The Family Key. I got three boxes of shells. Then, I took dad's shotgun off the wall in the pine room, his favorite duck gun, a 12-gauge Remington 1100 automatic. Taking out the plug, I went into the living room. I placed a chair against the door. Then, I turned over the couch and placed it in a corner. I got down behind it. Crouched, I held ready for anyone who might come up those steps.

Horrendous visions plowed through my mind. What if they set the steps at both ends of our apartment on fire? In all those old desert movies which I had been watching on television, the Sudanese and other hordes of evil blacks had overrun the whites in their valiant efforts to defend their outposts.

I would be just one more.

It would be worse than when the tornado had hit Ravenna.

Several hours passed. I tried to remain vigilant but fell asleep, holding the butcher knife in one hand and the 22 in the other. When the first gray of dawn appeared, I went to mom and dad's window.

Irvine was a ghost town.

Then, something caught my eye, a piece of cardboard with black printing on it. Straight across the street. Propped up in a high shoeshine chair in front of the Riverview Hotel. The old chair stood just off to the left of the main entrance. Irvine knew that chair. There was an ageless little black man who lived in the basement of that hotel. Had one tiny room to lay in. Made his keep by trying to remove Irvine's filth off its shoes. He wasn't much bigger than the black lawn jockey statues in the yards up and down those Main Street houses. Nobody knew his real name, or cared. They called him, "Lightning. "

Lightning knew his place.

Harmless. Liked a little drink. Shoplifted. But, he knew his place.

I stood reading the sign. The lettering was large and uneven:

    GON SOWT FOR WINNER BE BAK NX YER LITNG

The blacks never did come.

Irvine was disappointed.

Many years have gone by since that night. On occasion I go back thru Irvine. The bridge and theater are still standing. I cannot help but own a special feeling when I see them. And I cannot help but remember that night when now I see a new sign:

"WELCOME TO IRVINE---MAY YOUR STAY BE PLEASANT."

4. White Starling

AUTHOR'S NOTE:
Mozart purchased a starling and kept it for a pet. He loved the bird's ability to mimic his music. When the bird died in June 1787, he wrote a poem that begins as such, "A little fool lies here, Whom I held dear."

———————————————————————

He was an old man. Skinny. Kept himself clean. Wore a long sleeved, starched khaki shirt with an "EKU" patch on the shoulder. Bald. But you never knew it. Baseball caps. Turtle necked. A drunk's eyes. Took his teeth out at nights. Set them next to his dime store bifocals, worn billfold and razor-sharp pocket knife once his dad's. Robert was a fast talker. At times, believable. He wasn't much different from any other of the drunks which came in to dad's liquor store where I was a clerk. On slow days we'd talk. He said he was a white country boy surrounded by blacks. He called them, niggers. The word was nothing to him. He'd been raised that way. Said, he'd just as soon shoot a foreigner as a nigger. And meant it. But Robert wasn't mean. He'd sometimes talk mean. Pretend mean. Almost convince himself he was mean. But he couldn't be. Wasn't in him. At heart, he was always just that little boy on the river down at Valley View. Looking at jellyfish floating around in the summer Kentucky River. Catching that gold, blue poka-dotted eel, he swore he once caught out of the river.

Robert didn't live far from our small liquor store. Worked nights for Eastern Kentucky University. Janitor. Ashamed he couldn't read. Illiterate and working at a University. He thought of himself as he thought others thought of him: He was nobody.

Just a white starling.

He had an affinity for Hiram Walker flavored brandies. Especially the half pints owning those pictures of peaches on the label. You didn't have to know reading to know those. He'd lean over the counter and point at them.

Born on a farm down at Valley View, picturesque area along the Kentucky River, he'd been the only child. His father had died before I got to know him. His mother soon after. He still owed on her funeral. I knew. I read Robert's mail. I was his interpreter to another world. That world of writing. That world of pride. He never talked religion. Saw me as a soft person to tap when in need.

And Robert stayed in need.

He lived at the very end of East Irvine Street in Richmond, Kentucky; it was Appalachia's dark alley of failure. Murders of every hue. Everything was stolen. Whatever you stole got stolen. An alley where nobody threw anything away, except cigarette butts, beer cans and their souls.

Bodies on the tracks. Bodies in garbage. Honky Tonks. Curs.
Dead bodies alive, alive bodies dead. On the other end of East Irvine was the Baptist church. On Sunday, East Irvine sobered. Bodies were in the weeds. But mostly, East Irvine sobered.

Robert, too.

He had tried to bring a bit of Valley View with him when he moved to East Irvine. A silver maple. Dogs. Chickens. A garden.
Everything but the river.

And it was the river he needed most.

Like anyone raised on the water it had done something to him.
Mother's milk in the form of liquid jade. The soul's checkmate.
What few white people there were on East Irvine were either owners in the liquor business or shrews.

Robert was the sole exception.

The blacks didn't bother him. Not much. That addled woman which sometimes lived with him, loved her double barrel shotgun. Just as apt to shoot Robert as anything else that moved in the yard. A few times the blacks had tried to steal Robert's chickens and pigeons.

Never again.

Robert winked whenever she was mentioned.

One of Robert's stories was about him getting dunked down on Silver Creek. He couldn't swim. When he got out on the bank, he claimed he shot the guy that dunked him in the belly with a .22 rifle. Killed him.

That was Robert.

Robert's woman was country gray. Hated people. On parole after killing three white men down at Valley View. That was her story. She was Robert's cousin. His only kinfolk on earth. She had nothing but him. Nothing.

He told people that she was his wife.

One August, Robert and I drove to The Kentucky State Fair. He drove. Couldn't read so I gave instructions. Couldn't read but was smart. Sharp memory. At sixty-five, still that boy down at Valley View. Storytelling. Wiry. Chasing women. Drinking. Knife playing. On our way, Robert and I began drinking something fierce, straight out of a quart of Gordon's Gin, chasing it with 7-UP. By the time we got a few miles out of town, approaching a downward curve leading to nearly 500' tall Clay's Ferry Bridge, he showed me what his 307 Malibu could do.

Buried the speedometer.

We laughed.

Coming home, I suspected Robert having lied when he said he bought two pigeons with the money I had given him. Inspecting the box in the back seat, revealed over a dozen stolen birds.

I took a drink.

Robert smiled.

All breeds of pigeons: Nunns. Fantails. Frills. Giant Homers. Lahores. Rollers.

I didn't ask questions.

He loved them.

It must be wonderful to fly. To leave the earth. Go wherever.

Go back to Valley View.

A few months later, I took him to The National Young Bird Show in Louisville. The biggest show in the United States for all different breeds of pigeons which are under a year old. I brought him to help me coop my racing homers. Feed. Water. Watch for thieves. He knew which ones were mine. I used dried pine needles for llter. In return, I paid for all his expenses. Liquor. And money to buy more pigeons. It wasn't long before the show secretary spoke over the loud speaker. Pigeons of different breeds were being stolen. If they caught who it was, they would prosecute to the fullest extent of the law.

Robert was nowhere to be found.

At last, I spotted him. Walking in between the rows of cages. A certain grace about his gait. Just that innocent boy down at Valley View. Headed to Sunday School.

I didn't bother asking him if he was guilty.

I explained the importance of his not being caught. It would be the end of us. Please stay away from the homing pigeons. My friends were there.

Stealing their pigeon was worse than stealing their wife.

That evening, Robert and I stayed in The Executive Inn with another fancier from St. Louis, Jim Goldschmidt. He was young, ambitious, strong and red headed. Jim bet Robert five dollars he couldn't kill a pint of Wild Turkey 101. A half minute later, Robert cut loose with a Rebel Yell collecting five dollars.

Jim wasn't satisfied.

When Robert wasn't watching, Jim poured a coke in Robert's empty bottle. Declared killing a pint was nothing. Downing its contents. Jim produced another pint. One which was genuine.

Another five-dollar bet was issued.

Robert smiled. Scooted the furniture. Announced his old age. Performed a cartwheel. Petted the bottle.

I took the whiskey. I wasn't about to watch him kill himself. I gave him five dollars. He had nothing to prove.

Robert felt fine. Claimed liquor never phased him. Five minutes later, he was drunk, pillow fighting, throwing mattresses.

An hour later, passed out.

Jim lay next to him, snoring. Bedsheets entwined over their clothed bodies.

I turned off the lights. During Johnnie Carson's monologue, Robert vomited. Erupted on a wall, himself, the bed, the sheets and Jim.

Jim woke. "OH MY GOD, YOU OL' BASTARD!"

The stench of puke filled the room. Bits of cheeseburger and 101.
Jim grabbed an edge of their mattress, yanking. Robert stopped dry-heaving, flying off into a crack like space between their bed and bathroom wall.

Robert's head emerged just in time to receive the mattress, sheets and pillow dumped atop him.

Nothing stirred for some time. Then, Robert crawled out finding refuge at the commode. He gazed at his reflection in the bowl until daybreak.

Morning broke with a glint of frost. We sat at breakfast among the legends in the racing homer world. Robert was hungover. Told me he wanted a quart of buttermilk.

Nothing else.

Buttermilk cures anything.

That day, Robert never made the pigeon scene. Goldshmidt reported, before leaving, he spotted Robert hanging his head out of my van, drinking another quart of buttermilk.

When night came, I found Robert in our cleaned room. Occasionally, a commercial plane would fly low over. Robert looked out the window in amazement. When the lights were off, Robert lay in his bed complaining of his condition. I asked him, what did he do before working at Eastern.

"Me and Pa were grave diggers. Dug ten straight years. Then, I had to dig one for Pa."

"Where did you dig graves?"

"For the government. Pa had a contract. We dug all the graves in The Blue Grass Army Depot and put them in another cemetery."

"Ever find anything interesting?"

"Most the times, the coffins were rotten. We'd put the bones in another box and bury it. We found a glass coffin and a brass coffin. Sometimes we'd find gold teeth. In one, there was the prettiest diamond you ever see-d."

I turned on the light and looked at Robert. "What did you do with it?"

"I put it in one of them boxes and buried it."

"How large was it?"

"Bigger than your thumbnail."

"You sure?"

"Yes sir. Our supervisor made a fuss over it."

"Do you remember where you buried it?"

"Sure do."

The next day, Robert and I walked through an isolated graveyard. Thirty-foot white pines surrounded the area. Robert had planted them when they were babies. Coming to a tombstone, Robert stopped. Told me, this was the one. I knelt beside the stone to read:

MARY ELIZABETH HALL
BORN 1762
DIED 1783
DEAR WIFE

My mind raced. "How deep is that box?"

"Three feet. Straight down."

"Robert, if I come back and dig, there better be a damn diamond!"

"It's there."

"If it's there, you'll get a case of peach brandy."

That Halloween night, I was back. A full moon. Wind caressed the pines. Alone, I turned on my frog light and began to dig. The ground was hard. Grass. Roots. Fifteen minutes later, soft dirt. At waist deep, I hit something.

A stone.

A foot marker.

As I bent over to pull the stone from the earth I sensed something odd.

"G R R R R."

Reflexing, I clinched my fist. I turned. At the edge of the grave was a large dog. "GET OUTTA HERE!"

The dog disappeared.

I stared at the tombstone and then up at the moon. All was surreal. Nothing was in the grave, except me.

The next day, Robert came. We went over his story. Concluded, his supervisor stole the box with the diamond. That year after I quit the store, I heard, Robert upped and died. Sickness lasted only a couple of days.

I went to see the addled woman and check on Robert's pigeons.

A heavy snow was on.

The 307 set on four flats.

No one was home, the doors wide open,

And not a bird to be found. Except one.

A starling.

It had somehow gotten trapped inside Robert's pigeon coop. I caught the bird and sat on Robert's open back porch. Everything was different, now.

No tales to tell.

No laughing.

Robert was gone.

I cried.

I couldn't stop.

Part of me had vanished.

I stepped out into the middle of the yard. The sky was blank gray.

I released the bird.

Watched it disappear.

I knew where it went.

It had to.

5. HELLO 49ER!

Back in the 1970's, when I was writing for THE IRVINE TIMES-HERALD, in Irvine, Kentucky, I heard about a man that lived out in the country which owned a small grocery store on the Winchester Road. His name was Shirley King, and he had been on the PT boat with John Kennedy during World War Two. Having grown up in the 1950's and 60's, it was impossible not to have heard of John Kennedy. And my grandfather, Daddy-Mack, was the owner of our small town's one picture show, where I had seen the movie, PT 109, starring Cliff Robertson, three times.

I grabbed my camera and some rolls of film, which our poor newspaper barely afforded, and jumped into my van and drove through Main Street, going past my old high school and out along the curvy Winchester Road which soon had me in the countryside.

I began seeing the late summer of goldenrod and goldfinches as the sun-and-shadows played with my mind. I continued driving until I came to a stretch where I spotted a grey, wooden building owning corrugated sheets of rust around its base, faded "RC COLA" advertisement signs on its side, and out front, "KING'S GROCERY." Entering, I found myself in a stagnant den of dim-lit, wooden shelves loaded in various canned goods. And on the floor, stacked against those counters, burlap commodities which my beloved Estill County so desperately sought. This place, I thought, was one of those begotten outposts so often robbed.

Back off in the store, in a corner behind the counters, a man in coveralls and a worn farmer's cap was messing around, acting like he was paying me little notice. A minute or so passed and then the man spoke, "Do you need anything?"

"I'm a writer," I answered. "I'm here, because I would like to do a story on a man named Shirley King. I'd like to know what he did with Kennedy during World War Two?"

"I'm Shirley King," spoke the man, grabbing a chunk of quiet.

I could somehow see that I had hit on a subject which took a hold on him. His stare went straight out the door to a world of long ago.

He stepped back from behind the counter. And though he was dressed like some farmer just in from fixing fences, I sensed, there was more to him than a barn full of tobacco or a cow having lost her calf. He looked a lot like the movie star, William Holden. Having grown up in a small apartment over the top of my grandfather's theater, I had developed the habit of identifying people by the way

movie stars looked and acted. For me,
Shirley King looked like a lonely William Holden.

"Kennedy was younger than any of us," spoke Shirley. "We called him, "Uncle Jack," He might have gone 120 pounds. We weren't on the 109. Ours was 49."

"49?"

"Yeah, that PT boat came after the 109. We called her 49. Joked, it would be 1949 before the war was over. PT stood for patrol torpedo. Motor patrol torpedo boats. They were supposed to get in close to torpedo ships. But it didn't take long before the Navy found out, PT boats were useless. They'd get blown up long before they could do anything. Our boat was one of the few that ever torpedoed a ship. Unfortunately, that ship, was ours, The Capella. It was an accident, on a training run. off Narragansett Bay."

"What was Kennedy like?"

"I liked him. Uncle Jack said, he loved to hear me talk. I guess, he enjoyed hearing a hillbilly. Late in '43, we had our torpedo tubes removed and replaced with mounted machine guns."

"How did the rest of the crew like a hillbilly?"

"The boys liked me just fine. They loved everything about Kentucky. You see, I kept a still on the boat. The Navy had this stuff called "Pink Lady" which was used to propel torpedoes; they put that pink stuff in it to keep us from drinking it. But After '43, we never had any torpedoes. Kennedy knew that. But Uncle Jack kept right on requisitioning "Pink Lady." I'd run it through my still and what came out would make you slap your grandma; made a smooth drink when you mixed it with pineapple juice. Some liked it with coconut. But I preferred it just like Uncle Jack did --- straight. After we'd lower the flag in the evenings, it was Pink Lady time."

"Did he ever talk about the 109?"

"Uncle Jack said, if he hadn't swum in college he'd-a never been able to save one guy. Some of our crew on 49 had been with him on 109. Kennedy's back hurt all the time. He allowed he'd had trouble with it even before 109; after what happened in that wreck, never helped any. We'd take 49 and go up and in and around these little islands and he'd never let us go any place where we couldn't fast turnaround. I guess 109 made him like that."

"What was the biggest event on the 49?"

"We saved forty marines one night. You should have seen them. Their boat had sunk just off shore. God knows what would have happened if we hadn't come along. The island was loaded with Japs. I pulled one marine in out of the water and he kissed me. Got them all on our boat and after we had them out of trouble we ran out of gas. Luckily, another PT Boat threw us a line and towed us back to Lambu Lambu; one of the marines died in Kennedy's bunk."

"I understand, you saw Kennedy in Kentucky?"

"Yeah, during the presidential campaign. Kennedy came through Louisville. He spotted my sign: 'HELLO 49ER!' He had the motorcade stop. Sent two secret service men over to fetch me. When I came up to him, he grinned and asked if I had any Pink Lady? I told him, I might if I looked right hard. He burst out laughing and got me to ride with him."

"Did you have it?"

"I'll never tell."

6. DEVIL ROCK

Odysseus managed to save himself and his men from the siren by putting melted wax in his crew's ears and tying himself to the mast making the crew swear they would not release him however desperately he begged.

 The "Devil Rock," found primarily in the Estill County, Kentucky mountains, in ways, is an Odysseus siren; it's Kentucky red agate, the most beautiful and valuable agate in the world, originating in a rare type of shale found only in a few pockets in the mountains, and sometimes in or along creeks where the agate geodes have washed out of their matrix.

On one of my first adventures hunting agate, I'd parked and hiked down an awful mountain, hoping to locate a certain creek and be successful. I had hunted for Kentucky red agate before with no luck. I walked over the mountain and into an isolated region, a giant hollow, knowing, I didn't want to fall or get snake-bit. Down there, I was on my own. As for the law, there wasn't any.

Once I got on the creek, I kept my head down; I knew what to look for, certain types of geodes with certain kinds of skin, to find one you had to concentrate, and, be lucky.

On this fine day, I'd lost myself, loving spring in a wild, deep Kentucky hollow. Alone. The tulip trees bloomed. The chimerical ripples on the creek whispered: "Would you like a red rendezvous? A gorgeous Marlboro red rendezvous, maybe swirling with yellow and black colors? A rock cut open so exotically gorgeous that few believed it was nature's handiwork and not man's.

I found myself on a horseshoe bend. The gravel shoal looked promising. All kinds of rocks. Maybe an agate? I cut across the bend, stepping over a log. There, before me, two other logs were connecting to two longer logs. I raised my head and saw what I didn't need to see:

Marijuana two feet tall. Thousands and thousands. Someone's seed bed, an operation on a major scale, my innocent mistake, worse than falling or being bitten by a snake.

At the same time, I stood by the plants, I began to hear noises: four wheelers, several. The hounds of hell. They were coming hard and fast. Headed toward my location. Possibly, to me?

DEVIL ROCK-- -- PART TWO

When Odysseus was blown off course, he encountered the wild Cyclopes who lived in a state of lawless anarchy. They lived without cultivating food. They built no homes or ships. They had no institutions or laws. They lived in caves and had no sense of community with others of their race. Their diet consisted of the meat of old goats, cheese and wine. The descendants of these Cyclopes wound up in Estill County. Nothing had changed. Except, now, they roamed on 4-wheelers, carried AK-47's and grew marijuana.

Lots of it.

DEVIL ROCK-- -- PART THREE

I only had a couple of seconds to do something. I could hold still. Face the inevitable. Suicide. I could try to run up or down the creek. I could cut across and try to make it to the woods. Or I could try to cut across the open field beside me and make it to a cave I'd once discovered.

Being innocent was beside the point.

Nobody from Estill county is innocent.

I ran for all I was worth.

Headed across the open field. Towards the very same direction which the four-wheeling the Cyclops were coming. Jim Thorpe would have been strides behind.

I tripped. Went down in the middle of the open field. Fell into a hole in the grass. I started back up but the Cyclops had broken through.

Four, four wheelers emerged from the woods. The Four Horsemen. Apocalypse. I dropped. Hugged the earth. The Cyclops didn't see me. I flattened out in a slight depression there in mother earth.

The Cyclops convened at their marijuana seed bed. One of them, Polyphemus, ordered, the ends of the earth be scoured! The four-wheelers spread out, searching in methodical, ruthless, Appalachian helter skelter, hungry for a capture. I laid lower than low with them crisscrossing close by me. It was only time until the checkerboard search produced my carcass.

One Cyclops, came within feet behind me. Two, once rode parallel along both my sides never seeing me. Polyphemus, AK-47 in hand, during in his foot search, paused a few feet from my head.

DEVIL ROCK-- -PART FOUR

When Odysseus escaped by Polyphemus, he did so by clutching the underbelly of a large ram. Polyphemus couldn't see Odysseus. But he knew he was there.

Nothing short of a gruesome death would satisfy. I didn't have any ram to clutch. I didn't have anything. I was just a simple agate hunter. All I had desired was just a fleck of red agate, a glint of the Devil Rock. I lay there in the middle of that open field with the Cyclops repeatedly coming ever so close. My fate, hanging in precarious balance.

I lay on my back, looking up; a buzzard circled. I couldn't see if it was smacking its lips. At long last, the Cyclops gave up. I wanted to inform Polyphemus that my name wasn't No Sweat. My name was Nobody. If they had found me, that is exactly who I would become. I laid there, listening to the Cyclops disappear. Only an idiot would have run straight out in the middle of an open field to hide. The gods had spared me. I prayed the Cyclops continued their search in the land of The Lotus Eaters. If they searched there, they wouldn't return; Estill County Lotus Eaters do little but dawdle and smile. However, some delve into politics.

DEVIL ROCK-- -PART FIVE

Eventually, I roamed through the woods, hiding near my parked chariot in the form of a van. I held dead-still late into the night, watching from an escapable distance, making certain, all was safe before going near.

I returned home to my beautiful, red-head wife, freckled and a figure to launch a thousand ships. I found no suitors; I was happy not having to string a bow and shoot through twelve axe heads.

The next morning, I found myself transformed from Odysseus to Jason. My goal was to recruit a stout-hearted Argonaut and embark on another perilous voyage to capture The Golden Fleece.

Not a golden fleece, a Kentucky red agate.

The Kentucky red agate I sought was only found in one spot in all of the universe. On a creek called, Middle Fork. Middle Fork feeds along with North Fork and South Fork into Station Camp. Station Camp feeds into the Kentucky River. The Kentucky River feeds into the Ohio River. The Ohio River feeds into The Mississippi River. The Mississippi River feeds into The Gulf Stream. And the Gulf Stream feeds straight into my heart.

I drove to South Irvine and located, Agateman. He dwelled in a trailer. If you got near his trailer, a wolf which roamed below, never growled, it chomped you in half. Inside a room in that weathered trailer, Agateman owned Fort Knox, the finest Kentucky red agate collection in the universe. To step into the room was to be blinded by red. I told Agateman of my narrow escape. After a blood oath in which I swore to the gods I
would never divulge his secret digging hole, we set sail the next dawn for a day

of digging; it was one matter to discover a weathered piece of agate in Middle Fork, entirely another, digging it straight from the matrix.

DEVIL ROCK-- -PART SIX

The next morning before dawn, I was back at Agateman's. As he invited me in, he began conversing, "I've known you since you were fifteen. Nothing has ever been real for you. What is it you pretend to do these days?"

"The job titles keep changing. I never last long. Anyone over me, finds out, all I do is write"

DEVIL ROCK-- -PART SEVEN

Driving towards Middle Fork, the sun broke red across the mountains. The world was red. Agateman geared down. "There's 60-inch rattlers where we're going."

"How come you call it, Devil Rock?"

"I've never known two friends who have hunted the rock for a long time that didn't wind up hating each other. Always a fight over who got what. There's been killings, but nobody knows it."

"How old is red agate?"

DEVIL ROCK-- -- PART EIGHT

"The Imperial Reds derive from the Renfro-Borden Formation. Early Mississippian Age. Around 350 million years ago. Kentucky made agate its state rock. It's a mineral, not a rock. Kentucky's state mineral is coal. Coal is a rock. Be glad we aren't packing in all the tools we'll need. I've got them hid near the dig. Iron diggers, picks, three kinds of shovels, two sledge hammers, an axe and two rock hammers. You've got your waders, don't you?"

"Yeah, in my pack. Do you think we will find one?"

"You never know. You could go a year of digging, all day every day and never get lucky. And we might find three, today. You just never know. But I am in good spot. I've brought some out that are unbelievable. You've seen them. Most have gone to museums."

DEVIL ROCK-- -- PART NINE

After a jarring, dirt-road ride into a seven-mile hollow, Agateman parked. I put on my waders and pack and was soon following Agateman's forced march up Middle Fork. Agateman cut off of Middle Fork and began hiking up a narrow branch which fed into the creek. Lagging behind, I was lucky I spotted him making the departure.

DEVIL ROCK-- -PART TEN

Agateman stopped as we continued to leave the branch and retrieve his hidden tools. I got the ones he left and followed. Not far, we came to a huge man-made hole in the mountain which ran into a cliff.

Down low, in the various formations, was an outcropping of yellow rock, the shale which held the red agate. I learned, shale was difficult to sledge hammer; every pounding of the hammer sending vibrations through my body. We trenched and re-routed the branch so that it helped remove the mud and rocks which we were digging.

It was dirty and hard work; Agateman would sledge for five minutes until he got tired. Then, I would take my turn, doing the same. At times, while Agateman sledged, I dug with a shovel, throwing busted rock and mud as far possible. I stayed stuck in the mud and rarely looked up.

Sometimes, we found ourselves tunneling under the cliff, following the layer of shale; it became dangerous; common sense dictated, a cave-in was inevitable; a cave-in of 40 feet of rocks directly above our bodies would only own one result. Still, we followed the crunchy layer inside the yellow shale believing red agate was close.

During special moments, the sound of the thud-sledging would suddenly give way to a ring-sound. When we hit this ring-sound, we stopped, knowing it was probably an agate. We knew, probably, we were not hitting a good red one, but there was always a chance we could be fooled. "You don't want to hit an agate more than once," spoke Agateman. "And not even once if you can help it. The less fractures an agate owns, the more it is worth."

Once an agate was hit we stopped. Then, we used a smaller sledge, a rock hammer, a pry bar, and the pick to carefully work around the outer edges of the specimen. Sometimes we found small geodes no bigger than a golf ball. These were easy to rock hammer out of the matrix. But the larger ones took determination. I had been with many diggers and was a fair digger myself but Agateman was a human bulldozer, knowing no rest or fear.

DEVIL ROCK---- PART ELEVEN

"How do you know if you have a good one?" I asked.

Agateman paused as his dark eyes scanned the woods. "If you don't see any red on the outside, you don't know, " he answered. "Even when you see color running into its feeder hole, it still might not be good. The good ones usually aren't round. I look for something, saucer-shaped. When you have a good one, it'll have a solid feel like a cannonball. If we get one like that, we pack it out and run it through a diamond-bladed saw. Agate is four times harder than steel. Some minerals inside the agate are harder than the others. If I think one is no good, I'll tap it along its fracture. All of them have a fracture. Sometimes, I mess up. When you do, it kills you."

DEVIL ROCK-- -- -PART TWELVE

Having hit into a geode which showed promise, Agateman stopped. "We should quit for the day," he said. "It'll be dark before we get out of the hollow."

We caved in an area to hide the geode and then left. We packed out several geodes which later proved to be worthless. The next morning, we were back with a small sledge and wedge and rock hammers. Around noon, Agateman stopped and grabbed my arm. He held a wild look in his eyes and whispered for me to be silent. The intense way his eyes scanned the woods, told me, someone was close.

We held motionless for a long time. Agateman had claimed we were digging on his property. But Agateman was an Estill Countian. Even if he claimed religion, his ability to tell the truth was compromised.

Crows are black, that's just the way it is.

DEVIL ROCK-- -PART THIRTEEN

I wasn't sure a red agate was worth dying over. After Agateman resumed digging, I spoke, "Isn't shale a hardened deposit formed in a shallow sea millions of years ago?"

"Read your Bible. It answers all questions."

"I don't have a Bible. I looked at one, once. According to scripture, the world is 5,500 years old. You told me, agate was formed millions of years ago."

DEVIL ROCK-- -- PART FOURTEEN

Back in our hole, Agateman worked the geode out of the matrix, and smiled. It was oval-shaped and felt solid. I put it in my duffel bag. We called it a day. After hiding the tools, we began hiking out of the tight hollow; the woods were fantasia: a yellow butterfly, trees rubbing and talking, tadpoles surfacing.

Arriving at an Estill County outpost calling itself a jewelry store, owned by a man named, Striker, Agateman and I walked into his place which show-cased worked down, polished agate fashioned into knife handles, belt buckles, rings, pendants and arrowheads. Agate and Striker were agate-business associates; Striker directed us to his backroom where his rock-saw was set up.

DEVIL ROCK-- -- PART FIFTEEN

The air about Striker's business had the nefarious odor of a green snake's breath. Striker smiled as his red eyes guided our fresh-dug geode into a vice.

Vice was everywhere, I sensed.

But this vice held all our dreams as the big diamond-bladed saw began slicing into our geode. "No Sweat, you still writing?" he asked.
"Day in, day out. Even when I am not writing, I am."

"Still on that outlaw, Ed Hawkins?"

"Yeah. I've turned it into a love story."

"He sure had the women."

"It's not about women. It's about his father and him. His father is a crooked preacher, named, The Reverend Moses, who leads the lost and misdirected."

"What about that other book you are working on, you done anything on it?"

"I live with it at all times, the journal of a lonely marijuana grower living next door to a depressed, retired SAC bomber pilot. I'm trying to keep it honest and call it fiction. Writing a book is worse than being in love. You can leave a woman but you can never leave a story. There's more to writing, than writing."

DEVIL ROCK-- -- PART SIXTEEN

I walked to a box containing our agate and leaned over, raising the lid. Inside, the rock-saw was busy; oil was flying along the saw blade as it sliced through the rock. I closed the lid. "I hear, Estill's new Judge collects agate?"

"Just the red," answered Striker. "He loves it. If you get busted for growing, he might let you go. Depends on how much you were growing and how good the rock is you give him."

DEVIL ROCK--- PART SEVENTEEN

Agateman walked over to the box, curious. The saw seemed to be taking forever. A half hour had passed and only a small incision had been made. He looked at the bottom; oil was everywhere.

DEVIL ROCK ---THE END

When at last the saw had completed its full cut, there came a distinct "THUMP" inside the box. The three of us walked over. Striker raised the lid. For the longest of time we stood in silence, looking down. Not a muscle moved. Expressions were frozen. Breathing ceased. Then, Agateman spoke, "That's the most beautiful agate I have ever seen."

"Me too," added Striker.

"I've never seen red lines come across the chevron, like that," I continued.

"Do you want that cut" asked Agateman. Or, do you want the next?"

"I'll take this."

"You've probably got ten thousand dollars, there," spoke Agateman.

There had never been such a contrast of deep black and Marlboro red. The agate owned hypnotic powers. I took my part of the agate and left for home.

*Post script—years later—As Time Goes By

The Cumberland Woman

Agateman had been digging   all day and wanted me   see what he'd found. Reaching inside his truck he unfolded a towel and handed me a bone.

I informed him, it was human. Nothing quite owns the airy fee of an old human bone. This was one of the two lower bones in our right arm. He took the bone back, wrapped it, placing it in his truck, asking if I wanted to go back to the cliff in the morning.

I spent the night getting everything ready. I'd been digging up old Indian skeletons since I was a boy. Back then, I was always on the front page of our local paper showing off skeletons. Now, that same stuff would throw me in prison as a looter owning no respect for the dead.

When I got to his trailer, I could see he was still a kid as he grabbed his certain shovel, the sifter he'd crafted, apples and oranges we'd eat during the day and a backpack which always held everything we needed. I unloaded my gear into his truck and soon we were gone. It was grand to be with my friend and sneaking off to do what we loved.

We drove along the Kentucky River where we'd relic hunted the plowed fields and then turned, going into the mountains, driving up the worst one in the county. The old road ran along the ridges and where the shadows broke you could see darkness for miles. We turned several more times, the road always getting worse, until finally, our turn off ended and we parked. It was near dawn and the woods were silent as we put on our packs and grabbed what we needed before disappearing upwards along an old familiar trail cutting soft, passing by and through an ancient bed of sandstone.

Agateman was twelve years older than me, 70. He was still lean and remarkably strong. Not a 70 strong but more of a 30 strong. An inquisitive person who loved finding what was hidden, the last guy you ever wanted to anger. He owned a fine smile and was the king of Kentucky agate having taught me about the most beautiful rock in the world. In kind, I had paid him back with what I knew about hunting Indian relics; he was such a quick study with an eye for detail. The cliff we were headed to was one which I had shown him. One that I had first gone to more than 50 years ago having been packed there on the shoulders of men long dead. A half century had vanished. The thought gutted and haunted me.

We climbed down off the trail, going over the mountain, stepping by a bunch of blackberry briers which snuck up from the hollow. A moment later, a few feet away, a grouse flushed, the same bird my friend allowed he'd jumped the day before. We hiked a little farther, watching our step as we hugged a ledge and then stopped, getting out our cameras. There was something beguiling about this enormous cliff overhang, a mysterious gravity pulling at you, giving your soul a home more than any mansion.

At the dripline, we set down our sifter and s hovels, took off our packs, watching the phantom swallows and fat drops of   water fall from over a hundred feet directly above, hitting and splas   hing near our boots where so many chip   s of colored flint glistened. breaking the dull light. Most diggers had giv en up on this cliff as it had finally played out.   But my fri end had found new success using smaller wire in his s ifter and going belo w the ash lay ers down into compacted, golden sand, virginous at first glance.   Walking to our right, we followed the dripline until we came to a place piled wi th rocks, the spot where my friend had quit digging.

We moved them and I began digging with my bayonet.

This ancient cliff had produced thousands of relics. Everything always dating to Indians having lived there 1,000 to 2,000 years ago: pottery, celts, and unnotched arrowheads. The bear's footprint carved in a boulder was still there but the old hominy holes were chiseled and gone.

About an hour passed when some sand gave way next to a large rock. I put my hand in the hole and began to feel something round. For a moment, I thought it was a pot and then I realized, a skull. I slowed down and my friend moved closer as I carefully brushed away sand from the skull placed on its side facing east to the rise of each day.

"AHH!" shouted my friend, jerking his hand. Something had poked the middle of his palm.

Sticking up in the sand beside the skull was the tip of a point which I pulled out, a long, narrow spear point with flutes running lengthways down the face of each of its sides. Beside it, was a base section of a deer's skull and antler, polished and drilled, the hole just larger than a quarter.

"That's a Cumberland point," I said. "Seven thousand years old. We've just found the oldest burial ever discovered in Kentucky."

"What's this, a pipe?"

"No. It held a person's hair back in a ponytail. This skull is a woman. See her smooth features. Going by her teeth and the way all her lines over her skull have joined and smoothed over, she's old. Maybe eighty. Maybe, a hundred."

As I laid on my stomach trying to take good photographs, I noticed through my lens: the skull was drying out and crumbling and falling apart. In a few minutes, the face disappeared. The thought that I was the person to watch this paleo woman return to nature held me spellbound. She and I had dwelled in such different worlds and yet our ends would be the same.

We covered the skeleton and left. Our ride back was full of talk. Nobody had ever dug a human skeleton this old in Kentucky. Even throughout north and south America, such a discovery was extremely rare. If archaeologists had made the find, it would have been on the cover of National Geographic. But for us, it had to remain our secret.

A year went by. My friend's wife called, crying.

He went up the hill to shoot a coyote.

He didn't come back.

"I found him," she cried.

"Feet hung in barbwire.

Hanging upside down.

Not moving.

Gun went off.

He's dead.

No Sweat, I feel like I'm in a dream."

*Final postscript for Agateman---After You Are Gone

What'll I Do When You Are Far Away?

Sliding by The Hemlock

Stopped at his trailer.

His wife hugged me.

She started crying.

It was early. She didn't know I was coming.

"Sorry, I wasn't here sooner."

"It's alright. I read your letter."

"I'm going digging. He said, now that I've showed you this place you'll sneak back without me. I told him, I wouldn't."

"It's Okay. You can go, now."

"It's not like I'm going there without him."

"People ask, am I going to move? Why? Why should I move? There's his shoes and coat. I don't touch them."

"If he was here, he'd be giving you that good-bye kiss. He loved you. Always talked about you."

"One of his relatives called. One that never came to see us. Asked, uh, what are you going to do with his agate and Indian relics? I'll take care of them if you want? I told him, they aren't for sale. They'll never be for sale."

"I don't blame you. The memories."

 "Oh, I've got memories. More memories than those rocks."

"He was always good to me."

"He loved you like a son. Thought you were so smart."

"He was the smart one. The best digger I ever knew. They called from the funeral home. Said they were already on their way. Bringing his ashes. I couldn't take that. I couldn't. I told them to take them back. He had a Will. Wanted me and you to take his ashes and spread them where you all dug at Middle Fork. Will you go with me to do that?"

 "Yes."

"Go on and go digging. I'd give you his sifter and shovel, only, the
law never returned them."

Three hours later, alone, I was on the wooded trail he and I had marked. There was a place where we had stopped at the edge of a cliff and had to slide down the steep hill by an old hemlock.

I stood there for such a long time, looking, remembering. I saw us sliding
down by that hemlock.

7. **Miracle on East Irvine Street**

"Van Gogh remarked, the color black did not exist... He was never on East Irvine."

NS

Right after Thanksgiving the blacks would always start on us.
None of them were subtle. Christmas wasn't far off and they figured, we owed them something.

They wanted their Christmas.

A liquor store is a funny place. Ain't no other business like it. Nobody comes up to a cashier at a grocery store wanting to know, "Where is their Christmas?"

But a liquor store is different. Every person who has ever spent a penny figures you owe them something. Especially, at Christmas. They not only tell you they expect a gift, they all but demand it!

Especially the poor blacks.

A lot of times, it would be a black person who I had never seen.
A lot of the unfortunate blacks, would hit every liquor store, asking, "Where is my Christmas?" Back then, there were about a dozen liquor stores in Richmond, Kentucky. By the time these opportunist blacks had visited each liquor store, there
was a good chance they'd be drunk, free Christmas drunk; the best drunk you could get.

But the game never stopped there.

Most of the time, the really free-living blacks would come at us again and again, "wanting their Christmas."
"No Sweat, you got my Christmas!"

They'd even try you out, after Christmas.

And when you'd tell them, you'd given them a half-pint or something, they'd scratch their heads and act blank.

Wonderful performances.

Right by our little liquor store, was a couple of large beer warehouses. Most all the beer sold in Richmond came from them; an acre of glorious beer was stacked high in those temples. They got their beer by trucks coming straight from the breweries. Those temples stood smack in the middle of nearly a mile of black shanties. The blacks who lived there had nothing.

But they could dance, sing and sometimes laugh.

My father really didn't like black people. Even though they paid his for his Cadillacs and Main Street house. Dad acted like he liked them, but he didn't. Brought up the way I was, I should not have liked blacks either. But for some reason, I did. Little by little, each black customer had grown on me. Little by little, each one of them grew to be just as human as me.

Maybe, even more.

I found myself quietly sitting for hours, wondering, how they survived? How in the hell they could dance, sing or ever laugh?

It was a miracle.

A miracle on East Irvine.

We had a lot of regular poor blacks who traded with us: wine- heads, bootleggers--None had seen better days. From birth, all their days had grown worse. You could always count on these blacks to surface from their holes in search for hooch; liquor was not a pick-me-up.

But just the opposite.

By remaining numb-drunk, the world was mellow, more dream. Being cockeyed, prolonged the inevitable.

God loved those blacks even if dad didn't.

There was one black who became my friend, as friends go. He was short. At first glance, he appeared stocky, but wasn't. He just wore a lot of clothes. All into the Fall up into Spring, he'd wear layers of old clothes he found in trash. His shoes never fit. Nothing matched. And, in this, he was perfect. His eyes stuck out like a bullfrog's. And with the small head he possessed, he looked like a black Peter Lorre. He rarely traveled alone. He was usually with one or both of his brotherly friends who also came into our store. One of them, was a big and strong, possessing clam shell ears and
the long face of a chimp. The other, was Mr. Cool. Mr. Cool, wore a Bing Crosby straw hat and sunglasses. He was a philosopher. They were wonderfully natured; sometimes after they had had a touch of the grape, about a gallon's worth of touching, they'd take to pulling their pocket knives on each other. Sometimes, they'd get cut, but they never attached much weight to the matter. It was as

though they were young roosters, testing their spurs. Their lives were full of scars, inside and out.

What was one more?

Back during the summer before I quit the store, everything was just as always; the loaded semis rolled into the warehouses; Peter Lorre, Chimp and Mr. Cool helped unload the beer. It was their spontaneous income, their El Dorado.

Every day, except on Sundays, they'd make five dollars each for their labor. Sometimes two eighteen wheelers would roll in and that would be a ten-dollar day. A long but in the end, heavenly day.

That summer, Peter Lorre, Chimp and Mr. Cool, began wearing rolled up towels around their necks. They'd have on a stained T-shirt, sports jacket, a long-billed cap, sunglasses and those stolen-out-of- the-hotel towels wrapped around their necks. I began calling Peter Lorre, "Hollywood," because of the towel around his neck reminding me of some boxer or the way Elvis used to be.

All three always took their earnings to our store, spending it on cigarettes and on either Muscatel or Wild Irish Rose. They would buy the stuff by the fifth which cost a dollar and ninety cents. When they would come in---and they were always coming in--- they'd enjoy the ritual of keeping me guessing as to which of the two wines they were going to select, pretending to be the most discriminate of buyers and consummate epicureans of fine grape. If they finally said, "red," that meant the Rose. If, "green," or, "lizard," then, Muscatel. If you studied that red and green stuff you found, it was a fake grape juice with a lot of rotten alcohol dumped in to it to give it a vile fortification. It's not a real or true wine. But for a man's money, looking for the best punch for a dime, it's the only stuff. One swallow was to realize liquid desperation.

That summer, we had a family of rats eat D-Con and crawl off underneath our store. The heat caused their smell to rise, a thick, sweet smell that even the bootleggers found intolerable. Our problem, our store never had much of a foundation; most of the floorboards rested against the dirt-ground. Sometimes, when a customer would accidentally drop and break a bottle, dad would hold down his thirty-eight and squeeze off a few rounds. Customers thought he was mad. But he did it to drain off the whiskey. He figured, since it always manages to drain, there had to be a few places up in under there where a person could crawl. Or, at least lie flat on their belly and snake.

After a miserable week of those dead rats stinking up our store, dad got Hollywood to snake under the floor, feeling around and hunting for them. In time, Hollywood came out with the remains of one large rat, along with a hundred maggots. It was hard not to gag. It was even hard not to gag a full day later after Hollywood had slung the thing over on the railroad tracks. Dad gave him a fifth of

Muscatel for his efforts. Hollywood killed the bottle, wiping his hands on the neck towel, forgetting the matter.

During that summer more of those rats died off, their cousins, I suppose. One rat's smell overcame us so fully that dad gave Hollywood a full fresh gallon of Muscatel for his retrieving. That bottle full of booze represented two days gone. Manna from heaven. It was a reverse symbiotic relationship between man and rat. Liquored living through dying. Hollywood shut his eyes. For two days, like the once unborn child, he could float again in a womb, a dark and mysterious womb filled with embryotic grog.

Two days of gluttony.

I didn't see Hollywood for three semis. When the fourth came, he was back out there, unloading.

Out there, dancing, singing and laughing.

As the summer bore on, little Hollywood took more and more to drinking. Where he came up with the additional money was never my concern. But little by little, because of my fondness for his sad stories, he became indebted to our store for thirty-six dollars. He reached that point, where his credit could no longer be extended. He continued to trade with us, but his bill was left untouched. An IOU at a liquor store is no more than a certificate of ignorance on the owner's part.

Any fool knew that.

Dad drilled that into me.

And any owner also knew, to pressure a customer into paying an IOU was to lose him altogether; you had to play him as you might some great fish.

So, dad let it ride.

The summer of pink elephants, benders, and binges faded to a brief Fall of toots and tears. Winter came suddenly. The kind of snowbound winter where the sky was never seen and the snow never melted. A merciless winter where I stayed coiled around a
small electric heater, watching old black and white movies on a small TV in our liquor store's backroom.

Business was always good up into Christmas. The weeks just before Christmas are more than three times normal. During this time there is comradery, giving and wonderful spirit. But after New Year's Eve has passed, comes the horrible, pawing, lonely month of January.

The ice month.

January is a curse word in the liquor business. It is the month of no business. Everyone has already spent their money on libations and now feel the additional pangs of Christmas' after shock. It was sharp cold outside. Our coldest winter in history. That winter a dead rat could've handled our business.

One evening, I learned, my three black friends were all holed-up in an abandoned two-story mansion built before the Civil War. A queer place, not far from our store. One of those incredible ruins that could never be built again which now had no windows remaining. Where the tall Greek columns are chipped. And no railing remains on the winding staircase. A once grand southern palace. But now, a roost for wild pigeons. A place of forgotten spray-painted names over pitted plastered walls. One complete, owning frozen weeds, dead along its crumbled outside.

My friends slept off in a corner in one of the airy downstairs rooms. In the ceiling above them, were carved ornate tulips. And near their resting place, was a mammoth, marble fireplace which could accommodate a dozen armloads of wood. They had torn up cardboard boxes which they had utilized in every way. Old Hustler magazines had been used for kindlin. For wood they had torn off the walnut door frames, parts of the stairway, recessed book cases and some rafters they were able to get from one inside upstairs' eve. They drank their red and green, put up their knives and
huddled close inside one box for it was intensely cold.

Over a hundred years ago, there had been a war. Their forefathers had been told it was a great war to free them. A Civil War. And the slaves had been set free. But to Hollywood, Chimp and Mr. Cool, it was all just some kind of bad joke.

A cruel joke inside a black dream.

They knew of but one war. And in as much as they saw themselves losing, they were slowly becoming victorious; it had nothing to do with them, living in a mansion.

Hollywood came out that freezing evening to our store. His eyes were red, his nose running, and he was shivering. He came in and stood by the bar just to get warm, but he proceeded to ask my father, "Where is my Christmas?"

Dad had given him his Christmas. He had given him several Christmases.

We all knew that.

Dad looked at me and then back at Hollywood. We had done no business that day. We had done no business the day before. Not even a half-pint. Dad's mood was reflective. By nature, he had always been greedy. Yet, always boasting the opposite. The pronounced veins in his neck swelled with the zero day. The backwards day, as he had called it.

"Why sure, Hollywood," spoke my father. "Whatever you want. I'll be glad to give you your Christmas. More than happy. Let's see, now. How about a half pint of Kessler?"

Hollywood was perplexed. He stood still for a moment. Then shook his head, no.

"No? What about a pint of Kentucky Gentleman?"

Hollywood paused. Then, shook his head, no, once again.

"No?" continued dad. "Well, what about that half gallon of black Jack Daniels, up there on the top shelf? Would that be Christmas?"
Hollywood stood spellbound, looking up. "You really mean it. You ain't just jivin'?"

"Why sure I mean it. No Sweat, climb up there, and get that bottle. Wipe the dust off it for my good man while I go to the backroom."
For a few precious time-locked moments, Hollywood and I stood with smiles. Dad had been caught oddly out of character. I continued wiping the heavy bottle. Hollywood began to believe in miracles.

Dad reappeared taking the half-gallon from my hands and stood it up on the cracked linoleum bar in front of Hollywood for him to caress, never taking his own strong hand off the bottle.

As Hollywood rubbed the glass, he starred deep into it, as though it were some crystal ball. His bug eyes bulging, nearly out of his head. Yet, there was a sleepiness that soon lay about them. "Goddamn," he said, in almost a whisper. "There is a Santa Claus."

It was a miracle on East Irvine Street.

Or, so we thought.

Once Hollywood finally quit staring into the bottle---the bottle which still had dad's hand firmly clasping its neck-----he noticed, dad's other hand tallying figures on the adding machine.
"Let's see, now," said dad. "Your bill, that you owe, comes out to thirty-six dollars, and I haven' t added on any interest. Let's see, now. This half-gallon of Jack Daniels, is twenty-four dollars. Is that right, No Sweat?"

"That's right, dad."

Dad climbed back up and re-shelved the bottle to its original position. Stepping down, he spoke, "Twenty-four from thirty-six, leaves twelve. Twelve dollars. Is that right, No Sweat?"

"That's right, dad."

"So, now, all you owe, is twelve dollars," continued dad, staring at Hollywood.

"But. But you---"

"There's no buts about it. What other liquor store would've been so generous? Can you think of one, No Sweat?"

"Not a one, dad."

Hollywood's face tilted down. His spirit was ruined. There would be no half-gallon nightcap this bitter evening. He departed into the freezing dark, allowing just a dash of chill from the outside as the door quickly shut itself back.

About a week passed. I hadn't seen Hollywood. Then, the next evening, around midnight at closing, another poor black person came into our store. I was alone as he told me the story about Hollywood and his two pals. How, apparently, they'd gotten bad drunk one night, and, how a case of empty half-gallons of lizard lay around their bodies when they were discovered. Frozen stiff. Lifeless. Huddled together in a box near the fireplace.

They had been dead for a week.

I thought long and hard about the three. About them dancing, singing and laughing. They never did have any music, but they loved to dance. Danced all the time. Danced to themselves. Sang to themselves. And they never did have anything to laugh about. But they laughed constantly. I kept thinking about the real humility they had shown. I thought about that summer before the winter. They were dead, now. Already forgotten. I never
learned where they were buried. I never asked. I'm not sure I had the courage to know. I guess those little knives are rust by now. I realize they won the war.

The only war.

8. FORT BOONESBOROUGH

Word spread throughout the hills: The University of Kentucky anthropology department was fixing to conduct an excavation at Fort Boonesborough, Kentucky; Fort Boonesborough was the most hallowed location in all Kentucky when it came to history, Daniel Boone's place of places. The Fort and all its surrounding area was now one of Kentucky's state parks, possessing wily park rangers on guard to arrest any archeological looters.

I had recently missed out on a digging campaign with some consortium of five New York colleges and Universities who had planned to excavate in San Salvador, searching for Columbus' first landing. Initially, my transportation, board, food and pay were offered for my services as an archaeologist. Prior to the dig, I kept receiving correspondence, relaying different perks were no longer being offered. This continued, until finally, I was informed, all the archaeologists would now have to pay to have the privilege of digging at the site.

I never went. Paying to dig was never for me. I had been digging and finding relics all my life. The thought of paying some college for me to do their work, was an insult. Still, I couldn't help but wonder, how grand it would have been for a hillbilly to discover where Columbus first landed. With this Boonesborough dig so close to my home, my heart didn't want to miss out; Daniel Boone was Kentucky's Columbus--I couldn't sleep, thinking about the excavation. I knew, if UK was going to take me unto their fold, I would have to put on a show; if Hollywood ever came to Estill County searching for actors, the rest of the world would be shut out; there wasn't a creature in the county that couldn't bark, hiss, scratch, jerk, limp, faint, bawl or own a spasm if need be, especially when it came to get a government check: I would have to pretend, anything UK said, was gospel. It felt odd getting up for a dig and not draped in camouflage. Not having my face painted in camouflage. Not having twigs sticking out of my toboggan. I felt, exposed.

I drove down to Fort Boonesborough. The top dog of UK's gang was a gal named, Loretta. Perfect, I thought. I could always bring up the day when Loretta Lynn and I once sat on the same stump and ate bologna sandwiches together; she even took a drink of my RC. I wouldn't have to lie about that. And, I didn't have to lie about me having a degree in anthropology, either. Although, when mentioned, Loretta doubted it. As she studied my long face, I could see, something told her, there wasn't one fraction of me, scholarly.

The pay for being a volunteer digger, was zero, take it or leave it.
Being from Estill County, I took it. This was one of those jobs I would pay to work if things went right. I acted tore up over no pay. I also acted as if any word which came from Loretta's mouth was good enough to go on the tablets at Mt.
Sinai: So shall Loretta sayeth, so shall it be done; mine was not to reason why.

Reluctantly, still suspicious, Loretta allowed me to be on her team. I bit a hole through my lip, for Ulysses S. Grant had just placed Robert E. Lee in his tent. Dawn to dark would be the hours. We had 31 straight days to expose the soul of Daniel Boone.

FORT BOONESBOROUGH-- -- PART TWO

On the opening day of the official fort site dig, there appeared TV crews as well as Eastern Kentucky University archivists holding their big cameras. This Daniel Boone stuff was a wonderful change of pace from marijuana busts and governmental corruption. In the first interview, Loretta spoke like she knew something, discoursing with the authority of Tarzan, explaining to Cheetah, what was going on. I recollected, it would be impossible for me to steal any of the lime-light. That night, I pushed my one remaining brain cell into a torment.

The next morning, I appeared for digging, wearing a brilliant, Kentucky cardinal red-colored, hooded sweatshirt. You could see the thing, from Pluto. No matter what anyone found or said, it was me, that the camera had to notice.

Hollywood archeology.

Vanity.

Estill Countians wallowed in the stuff. And, not always in the best light. One time, during one of the every-other-week-County--wide drug busts, which were always on Sunday mornings, the law captured more than the jail could hold. Got my sister, too. All the
prisoners rode around in buses. Somebody decided they ought to go down to Frankfort where they paraded around the capital. Had big signs on the buses: "PRISONERS WITH NO JAIL." On the way home, the buses stopped to pull through MacDonald's; 350 Happy Meals. Everybody had the munchies. The next morning, one of my wife's students interrupted her class. Asked, if that one girl they caught, was she her sister-in- law? My wife regrettably answered, yes. Adding, she did not think it was appropriate to bring up something like that in class. For a moment, nobody said anything more. The students could see, my wife was embarrassed. Then the student spoke up once more: That's alright," he condoled. "They got my daddy and both uncles, four cousins and all three of my brothers. Mom was scared to go into town to get milk, afraid they'd get her, too."

FORT BOONESBOROUGH-- -- -- -- -- -- PART THREE

As the sun broke across the Kentucky River valley, I found myself digging in a controlled block. UK had given me a sharp-edged beveled, small trowel; we dug as though every teaspoonful of dirt was gold.

I got bored as hell.

If the tip of the tip-end of a bent nail was found, our world halted; UK cannons blasted fireworks into heavens. Followed by cheers and a broadcasted analysis, converting an anthill into Mount Olympus.

God help us if we really did find something.

The TV crews scurried pell-mell to be near Loretta as she expounded; I had never seen a creature so full of herself. She attempted to cloak her character but failed miserably in the doing.

It didn't much matter.

Every night after the dig, I would go home and watch the TV. The red sweater was everywhere. No matter what stunning performance was put on by Loretta, that red sweater was the star.

As though she was never in focus.

She may have had her PhD.

But I had that red sweater.

FORT BOONESBOROUGH-- -- PART FOUR

At lunch the next day, the archaeologists broke for tofu and green tea; I had a bologna sandwich and an Ale-8. The conversation was dry, technical stuff, a heated discussion about "zone one" and "zone two." I snuck out to my van where Ale-8 was used as a chaser.

A wild-looking TV crew pulled in beside me, Channel 27. They were a porcupine on wheels possessing so many antennas. Some hippy from their bunch hollered over and asked if I was in charge. I walked over and let him have a little taste. "Look," I said. "they told me, if I was the ONLY person here, I still wasn't in charge. If you want to see the Big Wheel, she's over there, inside that building, explaining stuff. You can't miss her, she's the one wearing the khaki cargo pants and shoulder epaulettes owning those Kentucky state seal buttons, oh yeah, and a French pith helmet which has three peacock feathers attached to it. Her assistant, he's the one with the imperial mustache and smoking a churchwarden pipe. I'm informed, he can speak eleven languages, but he's never said a word to me. I think he's a German Yankee from Wisconsin or one of those other states up there that eat cheese. When they finish off their green tea, they'll get around to emerging."

The hippy newscaster took a big swig of EL TORO, my cheap tequila. I handed him the rest of my Ale-8. After emptying the bottle, he withdrew and lit a joint. "What are they doing down here?" he asked, forever holding the nefarious vapors in his tortured lungs.

" Slinging shit and getting famous," I responded, watching him exhale, the smoke drifting across Boone's Happy Hunting Grounds.

FORT BOONESBOROUGH-- -- PART FIVE

It would be interesting to know how much money Loretta is clearing off this dig? I'm doing the digging and she's counting the dough. I should have gone for my PhD.

 Another day of digging was in action when Loretta asked, "Have you all found anything?"

"Right now, we're in the upper strata," I responded. "We've found some early 1900's coins and screen-wire from the tourist cabins, built here after Boonesborough disappeared."

Loretta peered at me beneath that pith helmet and those peacock feathers owning a face of steel-disgust, then she walked away, disappearing.

"Does she know what she's doing?" asked a new guy who was now digging with me.

"Hell no," I answered, "She doesn't know shit from wild honey. She's got me digging, doesn't she?"

"How did you wrangle getting to dig? I was told, only the best archaeologists in the state are in on this?"

"Easy. I am from Estill County. I fed her a bunch a shit and she believed it."

"Is the fort really here?"

"Loretta has researched the hell out of it. Studied to where there's no studying left. Yes, we're digging the fort site. You can sleep on that. The D.A.R. put up a marker over there, I think, in the 30's. There's people saying we aren't at the right spot. They show us a five- thousand-year-old Big Sandy atlatl point and tell us they found it on Otter Creek. Boonesborough wasn't around then. Them Injuns they're finding, are the great-great grandpas of the
bunch were tracking."

FORT BOONESBOROUGH-- -- PART SIX

For a passive moment, the fresh quart of EL TORO, which I had kept hidden but was occasionally visiting, took a hold on me, enough so, I told the truth to my hippie friend, the TV guy who was off sneaking a drink with me: "My heart feels Loretta is plenty smart. Far more intelligent than I am or ever could be. Somehow, she knows how special this dig is to me. That kind of smart goes far beyond a PhD. I've tried to make-up for my ignorance. I keep attempting to make everyone laugh. It's not worked. I failed at being an anthropologist. But now, for a while, she's rescued me. It feels grand. So far, I've been four flat tires for her…Say, would-ja like another drink?"

"Don't feel bad, "spoke the hippy, taking the bottle. "I'm a failure, too. My parents wanted me to be a lawyer."

"Life is too ridiculous. Thank God for EL TORO."

FORT BOONESBOROUGH---PART SEVEN

That late afternoon, I left at the same time as everyone else. I drove the old road back to Richmond finishing off the quart. Then, I drove back to Boonesborough. It was dark. The place was deserted. I parked and staggered down to the site and sat down at the edge of where I had been digging. A queer fog soon set in, encompassed me in a cloud. I couldn't see anything; I began to pick up on the souls who stirred at the site. I couldn't feel a hint of Daniel Boone. But something was certainly there. More than one. The silence and fog held me. In a peculiar and unexplainable way, I traveled back through time. I found myself five-hundred years before Boonesborough, alone with strong spirits, alone with the ghosts of Indians. I could see them: the women were using bone needles, working a black bear's hide; Men were cutting the tines off a deer's rack, prepping them for atlatl points; mussels were cooking in the coals; huts faced the river. Not once did the Indians look at me. I laid down on the ground. The dirt, dust and souls touched me inside and out. I remained alone for the longest of time.

 When dark gave to the calm of early light, I raised. There were cars, parking. Loretta would soon be near. I walked to my van. It was impossible to tell anyone what I had experienced. A new day of digging was in the make. "We're going to find something
today," I told a young archeologist. "I feel it in my bones."

FORT BOONESBOROUGH-- -PART EIGHT

As the day progressed, I found French musket flints which were considered lower grade flints as they did not afford as many strikes as other flints; these amber-colored, chipped-square flints were often shipped in barrels to the Colonists. They had little value to relic dealers but for Loretta in her peacock plumes, she was ecstatic, realizing, we were discovering artifacts from Daniel Boone's time.

FORT BOONESBOROUGH-- -PART NINE

It wasn't enough that the TV cameras stayed glued to our every move. Now there were school buses from the surrounding Kentucky counties unloading students to come and observe. It was mostly a wonderful excuse for teachers to be relieved of their normal duties: Dodging spitballs.

Day by day our archeological contingent was growing legendary in stature. As we dug and conversed, I mentioned the lesser publicized history about Daniel Boone wherein his having oddly disappeared one evening with all the money entrusted to him by the inhabitants of the fort. Also, the better-known story regarding his heroic run from an Indian village to save the fort, finding in the process, after being absent for a couple of years, his wife, Rebecca, new baby. And last, the story where his own bravado served to get his son butchered at Blue Licks.

Nobody wanted to hear those stories.

I continued making fun of Daniel Boone: "It was peculiar, when Fess Parker portrayed Daniel Boone, he ran around through the woods with a bare-assed, Harvard educated Indian, Mingo. Something was going on there. Talk about your odd couple."

I tried not to mention the possible mistake which the state of Kentucky made when they went to Missouri to exhume Daniel's bones…Did Kentucky dig up a slave by mistake?

Is Boone in Boone's grave?

I suppose I was being viewed as disrespectful instead of accurate as I could see, nobody wanted to ponder such. I wasn't surprised when Loretta upped and decided, it would be best that I leave from the two main blocks which we had established. "No Sweat, it would be best for the group if you would go dig over there somewhere," she said. Her peacocked-pith helmet gestured off towards the river. I sensed, she really didn't want me digging near the river as much as she desired me, smack in it. And, somewhere cemented to the bottom.

I left the group and walked some 75 feet towards the river. Loretta didn't begin to know but she was doing me a favor. Being near so many snobs with stratosphere egos was hard on my health. Whatever malady that bunch was suffering from---my soul was desperate to evade.

God Bless You, Loretta!

As I walked away to begin a new excavation block, Loretta afforded me a fake smile, much in kind as the Mexicans must have given Davy Crockett after his capture and execution at the Alamo.

I looked at the grassy ground before me. UK's gang was behind me. I was alone and totally in charge of digging "Block C." Digging a square in the ground. Something inside of me was stirring. I smiled an honest smile. Knelt and stabbed the earth with my trowel.

FORT BOONESBOROUGH-- -PART TEN

There is this wonderful negative side to professional archaeologists. Even though they are smart, rubbing numbers together and drawing conclusions, they forget one small thing. They are no more than hypocritical mercenaries who term themselves, professionals. Those Hessians which were paid to come to America and kill our patriots called themselves professionals, too.

Washington's men called them other things.

It is queer such an attitude of supremacy exists among these professionals. In all their worldly knowledge, they somehow conveniently fail to realize, it is and has always been the amateur diggers who have overwhelmingly made most archeological discoveries; not PhD people who have made talk into an art. Not scientific politicians. Not PhD people who must have grant money before they will get out of bed.

Invisible blinders. That's what these professionals wear. The lowly looters are not allowed positive mention. The scum looters are mindless worms.

Fort Boonesborough had recorded burials. I mentioned this to Loretta. She told me, if I discovered a burial, I was to respect it and dig around it.

That sounded good.

But after I pondered the matter, I sensed her dictum was rather ridiculous.

What was respectful about digging everything up around a burial, except it?

Must bones alone be violated for the burial to be violated?

If I put up a Wal-Mart around the burial, was that Okay?

The American Indian Movement, AIM, had attempted some sort of conscience implant into the archeological community; even managed to get the Kentucky politicians sober enough to make it a law. Such was good for votes. Clean up and maintain healthy consciousness. Helped keep the politicians in office so they could kiss babies, steal money and chase pages.

I questioned Loretta as to why it was OK for professionals to dig up burials and plaster them on the cover of National Geographic and television? Even okay for them to dig up mummies and put them on tours all over the world?

Making money while "Being respectful."

She explained, "The scientific community does such with respect. It benefits man's knowledge of himself."

I never argued.

Her truth was way overrated.

The emperor's clothes were beautiful, weren't they?

Loretta could've made another good Kentucky governor.

Where did these professionals go to possess the power to declare what is moral?

Did the Pope sneak off and bless them?

Did their PhD transform each one of them into God?

I began digging, putting all the soil into labeled bags, recording what dirt came from what level in Block C. Then, that dirt was sifted. What was found was recorded. I stepped up the pace. The "living floor" of the fort was around three feet deep; this was
the actual dirt on which the Boonesborough pioneers had walked and lived.

Standing on it, felt fine. I stood where Boone stood.

FORT BOONESBOROUGH-- -PART ELEVEN

Several days evaporated. I began to lose myself while digging, hand wrought nails, musket balls.

Not much.

These pioneers were poor. Little trash. Made the hunt just that more teasing.

Then I lucked into a feature: a fireplace inside the fort.

Carefully troweling, I edged around the fireplace rocks, uncovering a hog's jaw, an elk's sawed antler, and lo and behold, a shard of redware.

The UK tribe had redware as their prime objective.

If redware could be found, its origin could be determined.

The first settlers to establish Fort Boonesborough were from North Carolina. If this shard of redware was from North Carolina, a link could be established. Future grant money for a major excavation of Boonesborough rode in large part on the positive proof we were digging at the right spot.

This one shard was the ballgame.

As I began removing specks of dirt away from the redware, I stopped when I had exposed as much about the size of a quarter. I looked up from my hole. Off away from me in the main group, Loretta was explaining stuff to the television stations.

I sent a runner to Loretta and told her to ask Loretta to come over to my Block C and have a look at what I had found.

The runner interrupted Loretta as she was being interviewed on television. I could tell by the way she was tromping toward me with the TV crews bird-dogging close behind, I better have another King Tutankhamen's golden anthropoid coffin before me.

Or something damn close.

"What is it?" demanded Loretta, peering down on me so as to say, she was a ten-thousand-dollar hawk waiting on a corroded-penny sparrow; all the TV lenses zoomed in and focused on me. Loretta, in the movie, The Ten Commandments, became Yul Brynner, Ramses, the Pharaoh, and I, Charlton Heston, groveling in the dirt; only, I wasn't nearly naked as Charleton Heston had been in that movie; I had on my red sweater. "I believe, I have found redware," I said, looking down at the exposed shard.

Nancy bent slightly over. The quickest glance ever in history. The TV cameras were salivating for the next words from the peacocked oracle: "That's not redware," she defiantly proclaimed, owning a command-display of total disgust. She marched away like Pepe Le Pew, nose in the air, that French pith helmet with those peacock feathers tilted back, one feather loose and nearly touching the ground.

FORT BOONESBOROUGH-- -PART TWELVE

After Loretta returned to her interview, I flopped back down into Block C and stared at the small area of redware which I had exposed. Loretta should not have been that blind; the redware was plain to see. Something inside her had cast a spell over her vision,

Jealousy.

Green blindness.

Especially in front of those TV cameras.

I continued to brush dirt away from the shard. The only thing on earth bigger and redder than it was my sweater. I raised up out of my hole. The TV crews were still zoomed in on Nancy explaining stuff. She had her pith helmet off and was re-adjusting that one peacock feather.

I was really scared to bother her.

The cameras were zoomed inches from her face.

She loved it.

I felt like Oliver in Oliver when he contemplated asking for a second helping of porridge.

Somewhere deep inside me, I found the resolve to send the runner back to her once more. I sensed my sacrifice in the making. I laid back in the hole like Bugs Bunny waiting for Doc to show up. I got my bayonet and began cleaning my fingernails. I glanced toward Loretta as she coldly stared in my direction, and lowered my head.

What a wonderful moment.

The gods were watching.

I was an American in Paris.

Now, I had never seen the bulls run in Spain. But for the next few seconds after my runner had again interrupted her, I am sure that what I experienced was nothing short of such. In all my fears, I held Alamo defiant.

The charge was closing in.

The TV crews were lost in the dust.

"WHA-- -!" exclaimed Loretta, stopping in her tracks, inches from the edge of my hole. I was looking down at the redware, saying nothing, oblivious to anything, cleaning one of my fingernails. I wanted to say, "What's up, Doc?"

But the silence was so delicious.

Nancy stood frozen. Her eyes locked on the redware.

The shard may well have been neon.

I thought I might have to get a blow torch to thaw her out.

The mother of all sucker punches.

Sucker punched by the king of looters who took nothing serious.

That same SOB Loretta had banished from her experts.

Loretta slowly melted down. Her face came so close to the redware, I thought she was going to lick it.

I wanted to hum, Little Brown Jug.

I continued cleaning my little fingernail. Nothing like a manicure during madness. As slowly as she had melted, her eyes raised from the shard, peering into mine.

I gave her my best Opie Taylor.

"It's almost time to leave," she said, looking up into the grey sky. "Do you think, if I leave this, it will be here tomorrow? Only you and I know."

Trust and worry were in fine form.

Frogs wearing French pith helmets rarely ask snakes favors.

"I see no reason why it would disappear," I responded.

FORT BOONESBOROUGH-- -PART THIRTEEN

I hopped up in my van and headed home. I felt like heading to the first bar. That UK bunch hadn't found dog. They went on about rules, laws, morality, and all kinds of crap. They failed to mention the thousands upon thousands of Indian skeletons they had in boxes in a tin tobacco warehouse. If that was respectful, then I'm Saint No Sweat.

I felt like painting Richmond red. All I had was enough for a beer.
I headed for First Street. Found Dave Billings, the owner of T-BOMBS. I felt almost honest, being dirty and all. Except for my manicure. One might have thought I was a construction worker default Data Placeholder if they didn't know me. Dave and I went all through school together. Got so many whippings that teachers missed days for getting tennis arm. His father was a notorious bootlegger, a wonderful soul. And his sister, well, anthropologically speaking, had the finest set of mamaphrological protrusions of any gal in our school. I'd get Dave in headlocks when we fought. He was like getting a hold of a pregnant groundhog. And we were always fighting. I wouldn't dare let go in fear of what the results might be.

Dave was almost a perfect friend. We only saw each other when we were drunk. He would never let me buy a drink. And he knew the inclinations and history of every college girl who roamed into his lair.

And many they were.

From foreign students who needed help in talking good English to the stacked blonde who needed comforting because her cat had run away. "Let me sell you T-BOMBS," spoke Dave, filling my glass to the rim with white label George Dickel and setting a glass full of Coke beside it.

The kind you drink.

"How much?" I asked, holding a mouthful of Coke and then running Dickel straight behind it as the Coke went down first and the Dickel chasing close behind. And then, quicker than Santa moved from house to house, a drink of Coke following.

It was as though nothing had ever happened, except a simple sip of Coke.

Dave loved this way of drinking. It was chasing the chaser that got chased.

"One million Dollars," answered Dave, doing the Coke thing.

"If I had a million dollars, I'd be so far out on the ocean that an SOS would be useless."

FORT BOONESBOROUGH-- -PART FOURTEEN

After a drink, or was it two, possibly three and maybe four, I had a marvelous crowd gathered around. Girls of every persuasion and delusion. How they had come to think that I was the owner of

Calumet Farms presently eludes me. But they did.

At least two bought the story.

David told the ones who doubted my horse story that I was professor No Sweat from The University of Kentucky. Totally in charge of anything that had to do with archeology in Kentucky. And, if they played their cards right, they could get an "A" in my feel methods course.

"Gals," I said. "One morning I woke up in The Estill County Dump. It ain't no regular dump. Toxic waste. Body parts. Sewage from Saturn. You name it. It all runs straight in the Kentucky River. My uncle was the county Judge back when the county got
it. Got a damn fine kick-back, he confided to me. I realized, when I woke up in that dump that morning, I should not have done all the sinful things I've done. I wasn't sure how I had got there. I was getting poked by something sharp in the middle of my back. I felt around and found a pencil. I decided then and there I should write mom and dad. Tell them how awful I had been. And how I was fixing to mend my ways. I was in the middle of a sea of trash. I looked over and tore the label off some juice can and began to write: Dear Mom and Dad, I wrote. Then, I looked up to gather some good words to throw together: Dear Mom and Dad, I wrote again. The words weren't coming none too easy. I looked over. There was a long-necked bottle sticking up. I pulled it out of the rubble. It was a quart, half-full of Wild Irish Rose. I unscrewed the lid and took me a big drink. Or was it two. Maybe, three. And it might have been, four. Dear Mom and Dad, I wrote: If there is anything you need, just write."

FORT BOONESBOROUGH-- -PART FIFTEEN

"What do you really do?" asked a redhead. The lime in her Margarita matched the color of her eyes.

"I dig. I fool with racing pigeons. I bet on horses. I catch lobsters. But what I mostly do, is write. I got drunk with Rose Kennedy one afternoon out in her backyard down in Palm Beach. Just her and me, drinking beer all afternoon. She knew I was a diver. I'd been taking the Kennedys diving all summer When Rose got about three of them green-bottled French beers down inside her, she asked me, what I did for a living? I'm a writer, I told her. She asked which writers I most admired. I couldn't leave Twain out.
And I threw in Poe and Tennessee Williams. For good measure, I mentioned, Hemingway. She told me, Jack was with Hemingway when he received the Nobel."

"Now I've heard it all," said the redhead. She left going out of the door where the Richmond Police hid like hawks waiting for us poor doves.

It was one matter to tell a pile of lies and have everyone believing they might be true; drunk though they absolutely were. But it was altogether another wounding matter to tell a wee bit of truth and not have a soul believe it. My spirit began to decompose.

FORT BOONESBOROUGH-- -PART SIXTEEN

Night and day. Day and night. Thirty straight days. You would've thought, all a lonesome fellow could think on, was Fort Boonesborough. That Boonesborough would be under his skin. That he got no kick from champagne, just Boonesborough.

Twern't true. Not even close.

If you're married to the most gorgeous redhead God ever created, and the ocean, you have no control on how you ever get to feel. Summer winds across the sea and long red hair have their beguiling way.

Fort Boonesborough was nothing.

I've always been lucky.

UK had paraded it's over paid, pompous gamecocks to waltz their ground-penetrating radar, flotate pollen, wet down and interpret a post hole, sketch a field rock and pay an idiot genius in Michigan $500 to determine if a sawed section of antler was elk or deer.

The parade wore desultory.

For god's-sake, no wonder my begotten soul absolutely owned
zero control on me homing into T-BOMBS. It was all an old looter could stomach.

Send in the clowns.

Loretta was thumping her chest before the media. King Kong atop the Empire State Building, peacock feathers going every which way, holding up a shard.

She became, The Stature of Liberty, holding up that thing.

Start spreading the news!

She. and in perfect character, she alone, had made the discovery!

Lord, lord….

"Dave, would you be so merciful as to allow me another Coke, Dickel and Coke. I'm ready to fly to the moon and play among the stars."

"I'm going to get you a cab," spoke Dave. "Don't worry about your van. I'll be here in the morning. I'll hide the keys under the floor mat. You've had too much, you don't need to be driving."

FORT BOONESBOROUGH-- -- PART SEVENTEEN

The cab turned out to be a van. So many fun-loving, boisterous drunks sardined in with me. "Oh, Black Betty Bam Be Lamb" was blasting on the radio. For the moment, I thought, I was back at Churchill Downs at the 100th Derby. "207 Longview," I instructed the cabbie, then surrendered to the floor, my looted head resting partially on someone's shoes. A smile crept upon my visage. "Roxanne, you ain't gotta walk the streets tonight! "I shouted, and then passed out.

We drove for the longest of time. I kept waking up and passing back out. I was on a magical mystery tour. I heard the words, "Clay's Ferry."

Or so I thought.

George Dickel didn't give a damn.

I curled up into an embryonic position. For a period, there was an interruption in my stupor and dreams of sliding doors, people stepping on me and lights coming on and off.

George Dickel didn't care: Momma had told me not to come.

But hey. Then there was quiet. I dreamed there was a starry sky. I was 20 miles out. I was coming in off the Gulf Stream. Marvelous, being chauffeured into port.

Captain Dickel at the helm.

Then the van's door slid open. Artic-cold air swept in.

Again, I was trampled by so many strange drunks; laughter filled the night air. Monarchs, heading home, I supposed.

"Clay's Ferry Bridge." I heard.

My brain and George Dickel were swimming together.

Clay's Ferry?

I fought valiantly, rearing my head upwards to a window inside the van, then pressed my face against the glass. My eyes beheld an awful apparition: The fleeting last part of I-75, running over The Clay's Ferry Bridge, headed north to Lexington. My home was now many miles behind me. From T-Bombs, it had been less than a half-mile.

Spinning wheel. My world was a spinning wheel. Yeah, oh but verily yeah, it was true. I shook my head, passing back out, finding refuge onto the floor, headed to Lexington for my second time since leaving T-Bombs.

FORT BOONESBOROUGH-- -PART EIGHTEEN

As dark became dawn I found myself vanning back to Boonesborough.

I survived Lexington. Two times that night I had gone over to Lexington after leaving T-Bombs.

I never went home.

When I got back from Lexington the second time, the humanitarian cabbie let me out at my van; there was no charge.

The devils of Dickel were still swirling. The old, long and winding road back to Boonesborough.

Rhapsody in Blue.

At Block C, UK was having a hoedown.

I felt like a motherless child.

 Block C was being dismantled. Every anything tagged
and bagged. Black plastic was laid over the remaining living floor. Dirt was shoveled back in.

My grave, they filled.

The tents were coming down from over the main ring. Ringmaster Loretta, declared, the circus at end. She looked at me. "I saw where Larry Kelly, that lawyer you said you once worked for, once made the front page. The police got him for growing marijuana."

It wasn't enough that I was dissolved. Loretta desired to dissolve any remote hint of good I may have ever done.

"Yeah, I saw the article," I responded. There was no mention about how Larry and I had worked our asses off for several months to save most of Estill county from being bulldozed by oil
shale barons.

Burn down my house, damn it, Loretta, I thought. You love it, don't you? "Did you read the caption below Larry's photo?" I asked.

"I saw him standing in front of the marijuana and the police on each side of him."

"But did you read the caption?"

"No?"

"Hand me the paper, I'll read it for you. "And when Larry Kelly was apprehended, he was asked, to burn his crop. Mr. Kelly stated, he did not mind burning it, but asked if it would be Okay, to do it one joint at a time."

––––––––––––––––––––

Post Script. Fort Boonesborough. Years later.

Night and Day

I found myself at The Kentucky State Fair in Louisville. My wife, Chesteen, was holding Lance's left hand. I was holding his right. Lance is what life is about. Our tree of life. Our grandson. I wanted him to have a good time at The Fair. I'd had good ones with my grandfather.

We went into some big room to see what we could see. There were all kinds of stuff. As fate waxed, UK had a mobile archeological display.

Inside, this trailer, there was a display which stopped and held me.

Time stood still.

Loretta's salvation.

There, before me, in a glassed-in area, like some large aquarium, was my Block C, perfectly reconstructed; every little thing I had discovered just the way I had discovered it. I held still. I looked at Chesteen as she looked through the glass. Like Block C she had not changed over the years.

Last Postscript---Fort Boonesborough

On the Waterfront

The years continued to disappear after the Boonesborough excavation, each archeologist having participated there eventually disappearing, except for Loretta.

As fate owned, she was asked by the descendants of Boonesborough to discuss her excavation. By chance, my next-door neighbor, Ken Bellafonte, happened to be at the meeting. As she proceeded to expound on her findings, Ken raised his hand, asking, if she remembered No Sweat, who had dug with her?

Loretta looked at him, saying before her audience, "No, No Sweat was never present during our excavation. He was not there."

9. PRYSE CAVE

Red Dog and Blue kept aggravating me to take them digging. They didn't know beans about Indian stuff. We'd hunted and fished together. And we were all from Estill County. So, I said, "okay." One of the places I had dug was Pryse Cave, a difficult place to reach; I had dug for over four years in the cave, going 22' deep and finding 17 skeletons which C-14 dated 3,100 plus or minus 100 years old. I had gained a lot of notoriety when I dug the cave. The University of Kentucky had even wanted to publish the manuscript I had written on the dig. But that had been a long time ago, back in the late 60's. Back when I was in high school. Since then, the times and laws had changed.

"We'll need a sifter and a long-handled and short-handled shovel." I said. "I'd like three good lanterns but two will do. I'll bring a bayonet and two screwdrivers. If we get into a fireplace, we'll want to slow down and hand dig. That's where you find the good stuff. I also find it that way with Civil War stuff, too."

"Have you found any gold with them Indians?"

"I don't know where the gold stuff got started. I had a woman call me up from Ohio late one night and give me a good cussing. She
said she owned the cave and wanted half of the gold. I'd found."

"What did you tell her?"

"I told her there weren't no gold. I explained, these Indians were all from Estill county and dead broke."

None of us had a job, or wanted one. We weren't smart. But we were smart enough not to work. Estill County smart. I told inquisitive minds, I was a writer. Red Dog was a trapper and into "agriculture." Blue was on welfare, receiving an alcoholic's check and government cheese -- wonderful cheese, which went well with bologna and Budweiser. Without saying it, we agreed, a job eroded one's soul. What infinitesimal souls we had, we labored hard to keep. In a way, we were the staunch vanguard against civilization.

Estill County's finest.

Blue's pick up was of some ancient vintage. Most it still owned some red paint. We three red heads entered it with all the expectations of NASA's astronauts propelling from earth on Apollo 13's mission. Besides our digging equipment, Red and Blue had brought four five-gallon buckets. In them, were two cases of iced-down Budweiser and government cheese, the mainstay of all Estill Countians.

A pint of Kessler and six beers later, we began our ascent up the north slope of Everest. It wasn't the north slope. And it wasn't Everest. But you would have thought it was. We plodded up the steep mountain which led to the imperceptible cliff overhang. The six feet tall eighty feet wide entrance to Pryse Cave. We could've easily been cast for THE TREASURE OF SIERRA MADRE. Never in the annals of man has there been such a valiant effort to lug four five-gallon buckets up a mountain. The total physical struggle which ensued at The Pyramids of Giza paled in comparison.

I was the first to reach the cave, my old friend. A half-hour later, in drug Sir Edmund Hillary and George Mallory. It was Red Dog and Blue. They fell to the earth. To look upon them was to know they had engaged at great length with The Abominable Snowman, or worse yet, drawing their first sober breaths in months. Blue's visage was all Opie Taylor. "Where's the Indian stuff?" he inquired, withdrawing a beer. A few hours ago, he had been bragging about his AA meetings, required torture to get his government check.

And cheese.

Red Dog looked downward through the rugged woods below. It was hard to envision an Indian carrying the carcasses of deer up and down that terrain. The beer would not be lugged back down, leastways, not in the buckets.

"One place is about as good as another," I informed. "I'm going to dig back over in there. You can dig with me or do whatever you want."

"Think we ought to build a fire?"

"Don't build a big one. If that one bunch claiming they own the place comes up here, they'll want everything we find. If a game warden comes, ain't no telling. It wouldn't be good. If you dig a skeleton, the law will take your vehicle, your house, torture your family and give you thirty days in the electric chair. We'd all make the front page of The Lexington Herald. They've been trying to catch me for over twenty years. I'm Jesse James."

As Red Dog and Blue started a fire, I walked some sixty or seventy feet back into the cool cave and knelt to look at the dirt. I had so many memories here. Some of the best times of my life. Over the years, the cave had been potholed to death. I wasn't sure where to dig. But something told me to dig here. I looked out towards the entrance. Red Dog and Blue were stretched out along the ground, a beer in their hands, waiting for the fire to catch.

I dug for about two hours. Red and Blue had finished off a bucket and were midway into another. The fire was appreciably too big. I'd hit a spot full of red ochre, charcoal and worked green flint. At about five feet deep, I found an odd bone. Roundish. It was human. It owned all the feel. A knee cap. I raised up. Red Dog and Blue were slicing off some cheese. I climbed out and went to them.

"I knew the cheese would bring a rat out of his hole," said Red Dog, handing me a beer. "What-ja find?"

I handed him the bone, got a slice of cheese and popped a beer. The government issued two kinds of cheese, white and yellow. Estill Countians are consummate cheese connoisseurs. The yellow had more of a bite. "That there is a patella," I said. "Its shape is what differentiates us from monkeys." I lied. Nothing differentiated us.

We stood as absolute proof.

"Where's the rest of him?" asked Red Dog.

"I'm guessing, there will be some big leg bones not far from where that came. If I find them, he'll be right there. It'll take me a while to properly dig him out."

"How can you tell if it's a man or a woman?"

"By the holes where their ears go. A man's hole is bigger. Men have to listen while the women do all the talking."

Going back, I began removing dirt. Off one way, I could see, the start of the femur. Going another way, the tibia and fibula. I settled down. A burial was there. Number eighteen for this cave; Lathiel Duffield at UK, had pondered hard. Most of the skeletons I had excavated were adult females. Why so many females? Was it a work station? Back in the late 60's when I had gone 22' deep, I just knew, I was going to discover something dating back to the Paleo era. I'd read so much on The Russell Cave Site which was very similar. But the C-14 date that I got back from a chemical research lab in Tokyo put it at 3,100 years old. All three of my carbon dates associated with burials at different levels were within 50 years of each other.

That one puzzled me.

Then, I realized, the people which had lived in this cave, had been carrying dirt out of the back of it and using it to cover their garbage, their burials and whatever else they chose; fifty years of accumulation would have brought over 20 feet of dirt out of the back end to the front.

I continued digging for several hours. There is something special about the glow and sound of a lantern when you are alone with a skeleton. Something special too, when you realize you are the first to look upon someone so far removed from the world you know.

Red Dog and Blue were deep into the third bucket. Every now and then one of them had ventured back to me with a cold beer and slice of cheese, checking on the progress. The pelvic blades were wide and high, a woman. As I cleared away along her ribs, I found a mussel shell half again bigger than my hand. The back of it had been cleaned down. The mother-of-pearl beauty it possessed was still lustrous -- a spoon of some nature. Next to it, a bit longer than my hand, oddly curved, drilled, splendid in the coloration of red, bone and black, was a raccoon's baculum.

"What's that?" asked Blue.

"That, gentleman, is a raccoon's pecker bone. The finest one I have ever seen."

The comments which followed from my two compatriots were most nefarious in nature. Red Dog staked claim to both relics. All I wanted was to shoot a few photographs. Of course, if there had been a 100-pound bar of gold, that may have presented a problem.

Red Dog and Blue went back to the entrance to fondle their new possessions. "SOMEBODY'S COMIN'!" yelled Red Dog.

I raised up. Red Dog and Blue's heads were trained, looking down over the mountain. Blue turned and looked at me.
"SOMEBODY'S COMIN'!" he alerted.

I couldn't believe it.

I almost went into shock.

Of all the exact moments, red handed, the burial couldn't've been on display any more perfect.

I grabbed the short-handled shovel and began trenching wildly beside the skeleton.

"THEY'RE ALMOST HERE!" whisper-hollered Red Dog.

I dug faster than I had ever dug in my life. Dirt was flying to beat ninety. The wall of dirt beside the skeleton collapsed. Covered everything. Including the skeleton and the lanterns.

I jumped out.

As I ran for all I was worth toward the entrance, I pitched my shovel over along a ledge and slid as if I were Pete Rose going into second base in between Red

Dog and Blue who had already positioned themselves by the fire. They were stretched out, lounging on the ground, appearing relaxed and yet concerned, looking intently at the fire.

I could hear a man talking just a few feet away as Red Dog pitched me a beer. Out of breath, I popped the top and tried to drink. There's something consuming about gazing into a fire and wishing you weren't alive. Wishing you hadn't done the things you had done. A five-second remission of your sins. I could only wonder; how many were in the posse? I had devoted 60,000 hours to a novel based on Ed Hawkins, an Estill County outlaw, who had been hunted down.

For the moment, I was all Ed.

"Hello," said a man around thirty years of age. He was city. He looked it. He smelled it. Behind him, was some woman. Just as green.

"How-ya doin'?" I replied, glancing at him and then back into the fire. Red Dog and Blue were holding tight. Into the valley of the shadow of death we're sure headed, I pondered. And with an ice- cold Budweiser.

"My father owns this cave," informed the man. "What are you all doing here?"

I looked at the center of the fire. Indeed. What were we doing here?

Suddenly, words just popped out of my mouth. I didn't even have time to think them. They came out smooth as though all my Estill County blood was on auto-pilot. "Lost our dog," I said. I took a sad drink.

A tear almost came out of my eye.

"What kind of dog?" asked the woman.

"His name was Blue," said Blue. "Best rabbit dog I ever owned."

"Seventeen years old," added Red Dog. He crushed his can. You could feel the hurt of that lost dog in the way he slowly crinkled the can. He reached over into the fourth bucket and got another.

"He jumped out of the truck and ran up the mountain. We heard him barking up in this area. We think he might have gone back in the cave. We've been waiting for him to come out."

"Blue is family to me," stated Blue. "I can't just leave him."

The man took the woman by the arm and stepped cautiously into the cave. Like a magnet, they walked exactly to the spot where I had been digging the burial. Fresh dirt was everywhere, easy to see.

"Honey," said the man. "Over in there, is where the archeologists from UK dug. Some man, named Robbie Robbins, looted the place before they got here. My parents would sure like to catch him."

Suddenly, two pigeons flew out of the cave. They owned a nest deep along the inner roof ledge. As the pigeons winged their twisted flight out, they nearly flew into the couple, just missing their heads. "BATS! OH GOD! BATS!" screamed the woman. Both ran back as hard as they could manage to the entrance. The pair of poor pigeons landed on a bare branch just outside the cave.

The birds appeared as tame as water.

I took a big drink. I'd seen a lot of things, but I'd never seen pigeons nesting in a cave. I had raced and shown racing homers all my life. "Those aren't bats," I told the couple. "They're ruffled grouse."

"Will they hurt you?" asked the woman, still nervous.

"Only if you get near their babies," I informed. "They must have a bunch back in there, somewhere."

Inasmuch as we may have been a detriment to society, and richly deserved to go straight to jail, fate spared us. In a way, we were a band of angels. We held close to our fire, story, Budweiser and cheese. The lament we displayed for that begotten dog was heart wrenching.

The pair of Buckeyes wished us well in finding Blue and soon departed, leaving us to console ourselves in our obvious sorrow. For a couple of minutes, we remained steadfast in the hope that old Blue would faithfully reappear.

"Blue, that Blue is one heck of a dog to run a rabbit up a mountain and into the depths of a bat-filled cave," I said, slicing off some cheese.

"Let's leave," said Blue. "I think that old Indian has put a curse on us."

Red Dog fished around in the fourth bucket for another cold one. "I'm ready to go, too," he said. "No use pushing our luck. I'm like Blue, I think that Indian has put a curse on us."

I was ready to leave as well. Not because I believed in any curse. I went back and dug out my lanterns and hid them along a ledge in the cave inside one of the buckets. We broke fire and killed the last three Budweisers. The block of cheese had been devoured,

Making it back to Blue's truck, we were soon on our way. A half-hour later, I was let off at my house. A cold rain had started. That night, I washed and went to bed. Early the next morning my phone rang:

"No Sweat, Blue's dead. After he took me home, he flipped his truck and went over a cliff. I want you to come here and get these two Indian things. We told you, there was a curse. Come and get them this morning or I am throwing them away."

As the American Anthem blared over the speakers and as I placed my hand over my heart, just beyond the reach of my six empty cups of Budweiser and my bitten cheeseburger with a piece of lettuce hanging out of it, beyond the large plate-glass windows in front of me, and out over and across the neatly arranged race track, the digital show of the American flag played magnificently on the screen which normally displayed Keeneland's hallowed Tote Board, a nefarious billboard having destroyed many wayward dreams of glory.

Finally, the honored and worn-out song ended, and I, along with so many other forgotten faces, drunks of the dawn, got to ease back down and be content that the near-sacred ordeal was thank-god at end. Somehow, I was relatively certain, Francis Scott Key had not envisioned his inspired poem being spread among so much scattered horse manure; HONKY TONK WOMEN would have played so much better.

But, alas, I was alone, as any decent writer eternally remains, drunk and of one mind: to win the first race and play on the track's money for the rest of the day; to be that rare and envied individual: "THE GUEST OF KEENELAND ON THEIR DIME," however charitable and profitless the verdant institution mightily proclaimed.

In earlier harmony with the pre-dawn Kentucky state bird cardinals, which were madly chirping out in the darkness and awakening myself and my family of oddly roosting buzzards, so strange behind my home, I had found myself gone, lost in the cannabis dawn, headed north on I-75, beyond all cares, barreling, Trojan-ferocious, occasionally seeing a glimpse of an actual highway; Ahab-steady-as-she-goes and whatever else it required to somehow amass myself at the horserace track where I had spent so many tainted formative years and where real men dwell and where the poor forgotten working commoners who drudge through another desultory counted eight hours, vanquished spirits physically absent, are left back, lowly in the mire of their mundane and dreaded jobs.

Only, it had been raining. Nothing like a hard morning rain with those 18 wheelers challenging your every hint of a move on I-75; each medicated trucker headed to Dayton, Ohio, loaded with god-only-knows and every mile a race for another dollar, and you in your old sports car, a mighty two inches off the ground, trying to adjust the volume and make sure the smoke doesn't accumulate and that your sunglasses are on just so and that you have two pens, one for backup.

Ah, but the gods were with me; why? I wasn't sure; perhaps they were enjoying observing, the self-ruination a simple Kentucky mortal. But then, I was beyond such rank thoughts and once again, I had the divine pleasure to witness myself entering through the pearly gates of Bluegrass's Valhalla, finding my secret parking spot cloaked among so many trees. There, yes, I departed from my green chariot in somewhat perfect Estill county symmetry on this good Friday before the 2008 Bluegrass Stakes, to whence all equines must be judged.

Soon, I was out of my chariot, smoke-entranced that it was, and trotting steadfastly in the rain towards the inner chambers of the clubhouse. Surely, no mortal would be seen. Just the perfect darkness before day. A time to have breakfast with the jockeys and maybe learn, something not on some poor program or form, that valuable bit of information, a wink or a nod from one of those small nut brave creatures, that gesture of long shot-sure-thing. Who knew, beyond the gods, which horse was sick?

But HARK! What was before me? What madness? Yeah, oh verily yeah!

TWERE A QUEER LONG LINE OF BLUE!

And though my eyes were red, there was no denying this line, this line of blue. My God, where had this line of blue derived? How could they already be here? Thousands upon thousands! A line-up, dwarfing any Cecil B. De Mill cast. Oh, how terribly wrong I had been about being alone! Oh, so verily mistaken! The cardinals had nothing on these pre-dawn creatures, this long, serpent line of blue!

I had passed them carefully as I continued my walk. A double blue line they were, as fine as Napoleon's troops headed into Russia, beginning in the parking lot and going all throughout the interior of Keeneland and passing by all pari-mutuel windows and rounding corners, and each person mustered in the ranks, proudly holding their two blue bottles of Maker's Mark, ready to be used as weapons if need called; all of them giving me a glance as I graced sun-glassed by, equally observing them as they observed back. Such a sight to see, those blue bottles possessing blue wax and nearly every person standing strong with anticipation. Oh, but certain, dressed in blue. Enough blue to fill the ocean, enough blue to make a sky, enough blue to break your heart, blue upon blue, the line pressed on, heads aimed in one direction, a silent blue siren held them. Onward blue, onward!

Minute upon minute I glided by the line with nothing availing me, thankful for being sick this Friday and unable to come in to lowly work. It would be a few hours later when my call would be made:

"I'M SICK AND CAN'T COME INTO TODAY."

"What's wrong with you?"

"I ache all over."

"Oh, that's right, you lifted a pencil, yesterday. It must have been a terrible strain on you."

"Yes, it was a big pencil."

Oh, but what a long blue line, a wagon train of blue people holding their blue bottles, each person a Conestoga wagon of blue, as though the confederates were invading and everything blue was in retreat.

Finally, I came to that familiar glass door that I needed to enter; the same glass door where the blue hordes were funneling; a man stood guarding the door on the inside, keeping it locked. I stood there beside my new-found blue stranger looking at this Keeneland man pecking on the door. "Sir, I just want a table. I'm not with these people."

The man was dumbfounded. In his misdirection and confusion, as he surely had no instructions for something like me, he allowed me entrance. Thanking him, I took but a few more steps to find my white-painted, rod-iron table and chair, where-whence I immediately began to place pen in hand and write the beginnings of my new novel, PIGEON.

But disturbingly, I sensed, something awry, and that mysterious something was close. I could feel a certain sprinkle of blue in the air, a cold smell of blue ice and a warm blue smell of summer beguilingly mixed together. Then, looking up, some twelve feet away, I looked directly at him as he was strangely looking at me. HE was the rags-to-riches reason the blue masses had lined up, the blue reason of all the maddening blue, yes, The Ward Bond of The Long Blue Line, The Legend, his mighty Blue Zeus self, Joe B. Hall.

GOD BLESS KENTUCKY BASKETBALL.

Every eager man, woman and child was there, wide-eyed to have Joe B. Hall sign their coveted whiskey bottle.

People fell out of rank on a constant basis coming up to me asking to borrow my poor pen as they had to fill out some official form which officially-blessed, that their bottle had genuinely been signed by the Blue Zeus himself, Joe B. Hall. And each time, I explained, "A writer never loans his pen. Without it he is, defenseless. Beyond his memory, it's all his got."

Each bottle metamorphosing from fifty-dollars to over two- hundred dollars at the stroke of Joe B's commanding signature. No mortal allowed more than two bottles. Each bottle carrying a serial number. The lower the number the more valuable the bottle.

Everything in perfect logic.

I started to put up a sign on my table; I would sign the bottles for $1.00 each. And they would own the signature of a future famous author. But I held still. There were two small boys being pulled on a blue wagon, both weary and crying on the passage. But no cry could deter this movement. It was Kentucky blue, bleeding blue, blue and blue yet. Let no man or child mistake that. Onward the blue line pushed. Each person reaching Joe B. and stopping to talk to THE LEGEND as he chuckled as though he were Santa in blue, telling tales of all blue manner over a blue-wildcat loudspeaker which filled our room, barely understandable, but it didn't matter, it was THE Blue Zeus! Blue vibrations filled the air!

Little Mexicans, God only knows from which villages, ran all about like so many mice in a barn. Each with some cleaning weapon; them dressed in the Keeneland beige outfits denoting their lowly rank with those sorrowful, green Keeneland hats and their little green lapel Keeneland insignia. Workers. No REAL green cards, likely. But then, that was the way it was supposed to be: Kentucky proud relished hierarchy. Each Mexican sweeping and mopping and cleaning, putting in new trash can liners, wiping the plate glass, two of them singing, making me wonder if they hadn't broken into my car. Such a delightful configuration of mankind in harmony; everything just as it should Kentucky be.

Then, the overhead TV screens all came on. On one, Martha Lane Collins, more square-shouldered than Dick Tracy, began lauding Joe B. Hall. "ZEUS thwarted POSEIDON!" she clamored, or something to that nature, relentlessly going on and on.

On another screen, Goose Givens, retold some begotten story between Joe B. and Bobby Knight. Knights jousting in fierce battle. He spoke of it as one might speak of the Holy Grail. "Long into the night we battled." Or something like that.

The LONG BLUE LINE held reverent throughout. Some all but weeping. One tall, sophisticated-looking lady, probably in her early 70's, hair tied-back in a bun, long blue velvet coat owning a blue fur collar, accidentally dropping her blue leather pocketbook, twice the size of a checkerboard, bottles hitting inside, extra bottles she had snuck by the Maker's Mark guards. Ah, Kentucky!

Little did the blue world know, the large bottle of orange juice I was drinking was three-fourths vodka. Florida sunshine engulfed in blue. I wished it had been, four-fifths. The ordeal was maddening. In a state last in education, health, income and more, everything we had whiskey, horses and basketball. I would soon, I imagined, see jockeys, drinking Maker's Mark while dribbling basketballs as they raced their horses through the Kentucky Derby A lady stepped up to my table and started to give me a metal badge. "Are you a Maker's Mark Ambassador?"

"No ma'am. But I am an Earl."

11. HEAVEN ROOSTED THERE

Hardly anyone noticed the pigeons on the bridge. That steel structure had dripped the colors of orange, blue, lime and silver, but now it was cedar green. Sometimes, I thought of it as though it were stretched steel dinosaur. And there were times, I suppose, because of all those intricate interconnecting braces silhouetting against the sky, it seemed like a giant spider web. I'd been born near that bridge and had lived there all my life and on this day, my tenth birthday, well, heaven roosted there.

The railroad tracks which I was balancing on, were a just short distance over the hill from the back of my little apartment. The tracks led under the bridge where there was this splintery telephone pole which was on a slope just up from the Kentucky river, flowing in its liquid jade-colored waters. That pole reminded me of Jesus' cross. Only there were boards up above that pole, a catwalk, running above the wires and insulators. Last week, at the base of the pole. I had propped a board.

The bridge overhead didn't go very far before it ended and ran into the Main Street of my home town, Irvine, Kentucky. Hardly anyone had a TV and every Saturday night my grandfather, the owner of the theater, played a scary movie for the crowd.

Tonight, his neon marquee advertised: "BRIDES OF DRACULA."

My mom was up the hill from me sitting high in her small chair at the entrance of the theater. She owned mysterious grey eyes and could look at you just like Ava Gardner. She always seemed happy and enjoyed talking to the customers and laughing with them while sitting in her glassed-in ticket booth. I knew she was selling tickets for twenty-five cents and that my grandfather was collecting them as the customers came through the door. Mom probably thought I was sitting where always sat, in the middle seat of the front row. But if I wasn't there, she had to figure, I was asleep on our back porch.

I had been planning for a long time when I propped that board against the telephone pole. The flashlight I'd gotten for my birthday was tied off from my belt when I lunged up the board making a desperate grab, the tips of my fingers just reaching where they had to be. I had dreamed of doing what I was doing and now that I was in that dream it felt strange. If I tore my clothes or dropped the flashlight, my father would surely find out. That, inevitably, would lead to a whipping with one of those leather belts that he had hanging down on the inside of the closet door in his bedroom.

My father was a strong man, an ex-Merchant Mariner. He looked like Robert Mitchum and ran a fruit stand on the street across from the theater. During the summers, every other Saturday night, like tonight, he would leave in his truck for Georgia. A few days later, he would return with crates of peaches or a load of melons and cantaloupes. When he was gone, mom and I were very close, often listening to Billie Holiday records. But when dad returned, things were always different, especially the love.

In the darkness, I was silent. Once atop the pole, I stood up, carefully balancing, stretching upwards into the hold-less air, my fingers barely reaching the edge of the catwalk. Pulling, I brought my body up and onto the rough boards and then rolled over on my back to rest. Peering into the darkness, I felt the vibrations of a truck as it passed overhead.

Turning on my flashlight, I crouched along the catwalk towards the river. Because of the slope of the ground below, each step was a gain in height. I slowly continued until I reached a massive concrete pillar which rose sixty feet above the river's edge. I paused to study the long shadow of the boat dock on the other side of the river. If I fell, my life was over. A bullfrog moaned in the distance and in that still moment, I smelled the faint smell of a pigeon, a light and powdery smell which sent a strange satisfaction into me, the same way a delicate rose does, only different.

Death so close for the sake of what?

A pigeon.

The pigeons on that bridge had been taunting my soul for as long as I could remember. When my parents were gone, I often found my face pressed against their end bedroom window. To get to that window you had to walk past that closet with the belts and past that bed where I was made to lay on my stomach when being whipped. I'd pull back those long and dark curtains, smelling and seeing the thick dust of the sills, and the gaze out onto Main Street with its turn of the century square brick buildings. Off to the left was the bridge. The pigeons were always there.

I turned on my light and shined it out along the long structural ribs of the bridge, the catwalk had stopped at the pillars and from there on out there were no holds. Such a vacuous feeling. I spotted two pigeons forever uncatchable. I turned my light back off and climbed back onto the catwalk and stopped at the first metal brace angling upward and out. I shined my light and there, in a small nook, gazing into my light, was a pigeon, light blue-grey in color, with two black stripes across its wings; its neck such a jewel of blue, purple, green and its eyes hypnotized rubies. The evening breeze began moving through the tops of the sycamores below the catwalk and for a moment my mind forgot about falling and thought only of the pigeon. I leaned out onto the brace and began hugging, inching upwards, keeping my head cocked while holding the light. When at last I got within grabbing distance, I stopped.

It happened as quick as the thought and just as true, the bird being caught. All those years of looking and now this. Holding tight to the pigeon's wings I shimmied back down to the catwalk. Getting better control of the bird, I was intrigued to see that the bird owned a seamless aluminum band on each leg. One band read, "AU 60 KY 6006." And the other, "CHAS HEITZMAN, JEFFERSONTOWN KY."

What is fate? What is it when two lives meet in a dream?

I found myself running back on the tracks. I stopped and my Converse cut up the trail through the kudzu to run up the sidewalk and enter past my grandfather and go into the ticket booth to show mom my pigeon. A small fan was blowing on her face when she turned and looked at me. I was the kind of boy that would always be lonely. But on this night, I owned a little of heaven. Mom smiled and grandfather did, too.

12. Whale Point

The airport on the north end of Eleuthera was about as big as a rich man's closet. When we flew into it, I was told by the natives that my luggage didn't arrive. It was around noon and I told my wife and daughter to go on and take our rental jeep to the house which we had rented some sixty miles south to Governor's Harbour, a swanky place, called THE TWIN COVES, located back in the jungle and secluded on the ocean. I told my wife, Chesteen, that I would wait for the next flight to come in hoping to retrieve our luggage which included my spear gun and diving gear as well as my metal detector. Eleuthera was settled by the English in the 1600's and the island is covered with the skeletal remains of English and Dutch houses from the 1700's --- a paradise for metal detecting. No one on this outer island in the southern part of the Bahamian chain cared anything at all about old stuff.

As I contained myself, all but alone at the airport in the typical Bahamian heat, I felt an Estill county urge to locate a beer colder than a mother in law's love. I had left the mangling strife of Kentucky some 1,200 miles north and my inner domain begged to keep it there. Attached to the airport was something of a liquor store no larger than a poor man's closet. Sitting on a chair was a native guarding over a cooler. The Kalik beer inside it, was $5.00 each. I looked at the quart bottle of coconut rum proudly standing behind him. It was $6.00.

Now, I was never worth a damn in math. The only significant accomplishment I can recall regarding anything at all to do with the horrible subject was when I led an expedition one Halloween night omletfying my high school's algebra teacher's house, vehicle, and husband. We spent a lot of money on those extra-large jumbo eggs. A whole case. Twelve times twelve. It was a glorious moment in math.

"Give me the bottle of rum," I said. "And would you be so gracious as to give me a cup of ice?"

I was just finishing my first large cup of rum when the next plane came in. Little planes, the kind drug runners appreciate. No luggage again. The next plane would be in another hour or so. The only sure thing in the Bahamas is that nothing is sure. I managed more ice and poured another cup.

I wasn't real sure about the metal detecting laws in the Bahamas. That's why I had taken my metal detector completely apart and placed it in several different pieces of luggage. I did know what the laws were regarding bringing an arbalete spear gun and that is why I had done the same for it. I tried to make them look like something they weren't. Something innocent. A part of a tripod. Or part to a pole spear.

With my cup empty the next plane came in. Again, no luck. I did the only thing any Estill Countian could do.

I went back for more ice.

That quart was over half gone as I began pouring my third drink. It was stagnant hot but I felt nothing. I asked the ice giver about old stuff and he looked at me with pity. You could see what he thought of me. Not much. The last plane of the day came in. Short of the rum, again, no luck. It was past suppertime and I went over to a dirty old Ford van. It was my chariot. Not what I had rented but what I had got. I got in it and swiped the dust off the seat and dash. Nothing beyond the bare basics on it began to work, hadn't worked in years. I fired her up took a big huge drink and headed south.

An hour later, I was back where I had started.

The quart had been licked dry. The sun was beginning to drop. My gas gauge was kissing zero. I knew I had missed my turn. This time, I wouldn't.

In the Bahamas, you are supposed to drive on the wrong side of the road. When you are dogface drunk from Estill county, nothing could be more challenging, especially in a Ford.

This time, locating my correct turn, which was indicated with a purple painted two by four, I applied my sandal, engaging the engine into warp force. Well, not actually. But almost. I sped by quaint residences with the solo thought of reaching my loved ones before dark. I envisioned a return of brave Ulysses, minus the luggage. As I approached an area called "WHALE POINT" I came onto a straight stretch and met a taxi torpedoing directly at me. The fool, I thought. Why doesn't he get on his side of the road? Can't he see me?

Just seconds before the head on, I cut hard to the right and went off the road, flipping my van upside down. As I slid over an embankment, I could hear the jungle around me scraping everything. Downward, I continued realizing, the next stop would be the last layer of Dante's Inferno. I tried to quote the 23rd Psalm but forgot the words. I really didn't have time to say it anyways.

Then, the van slid to a complete stop, wedged in between two coconut trees growing precariously at the edge of a cliff where on rare occasion a whale is spotted. The two coconut trees may well have been the very trees which donated the coconuts used in my rum. Little things like that have a way of sneaking their way into a true story. You couldn't have guided my van upside down and wedged it in between those two trees with finer precision. At first, I had trouble realizing I was still alive. Then, I knew if I had died, I sure wasn't going to wake up and find myself on some beautiful island in the Caribbean. Yeah, still alive. Wild drunk. Hurting.

Looking at reality upside down.

Eleuthera often has those BALI HAI sunsets wherein the island whispers and calls to you. This wasn't one of them. As the sun disappeared into the ocean I found myself crawling out of the window. On the cliff above, a small girl was standing and holding the taxi cab driver's hand. "HE'S ALIVE!" she shouted, pointing down in my direction. My left side was in pain. The double-edged rum was helping me hang on. I felt like I was in a bad dream. I crawled up the cliff to the two observers. At their feet, I rolled over looking up at them.

"You are very lucky," spoke the taxi cab driver. "God has saved you for a great purpose. Another man went off this cliff two weeks ago. We never found his body."

"Do you know where The Twin Coves is?" I asked, standing.

"Yes. But I need to call the police."

"Let's leave the police out of this."

"I have to call the police. If I don't, I could lose my license."

Just what I need, I thought. You get fed every third day in a Bahamian jail. A small fish head. Raw. The eyes are desert. Fish scales serve as toothpicks. For just a micro fraction of a second, I wished I was back in Estill County. At least there, you could pay off officials and get out of a mess like this. All my Estill county blood wanted to run. I stood there in the dark like some early French missionary awaiting a Huron inquisition. If there was a rack on Eleuthera, I would be ten feet tall by dawn. I had to hold positive. I thought of MIDNIGHT EXPRESS and THE COUNT OF MONTE CRISTO. I wasn't sure if they had electricity on Eleuthera. If they did, I was confident it would all be used on me. The Germans at Nuremberg couldn't hold a candle to what I had coming.

In about an hour the only policeman and the only cruiser on Eleuthera pulled up. He looked over the situation. Measured that I had gone 300 feet over the cliff. Then, he asked, that the taxi driver and I get into his cruiser. I sat at my normal place in such situations, the back seat. The officer held my license and read it with a flashlight. I sat in the middle of the backseat seeing the backs of two human shadows. Through it all, I was still plastered.

"Mr. Robbins," spoke the officer not turning around, "Have you had anything to drink?"

"Yes sir," I answered, too drunk to lie. "I bought a quart of coconut rum at the airport and drank every drop of it."

The officer raised his head and looked at the taxi cab driver. The taxi cab driver looked at the officer. There was the longest silence after I had spoken. That officer was allowing matters to digest. "Well, Mr. Robbins, I am not going to do anything to you. It is so rare to meet an honest man. I knew how much you drank. The man that sold you the quart, called me. He said, you might have trouble making it. All I ask, is that you go to our station sometime before you leave and make a statement. There will be no charges."

After the law left, I felt like Charlton Heston, looking back at having crossed the Red Sea. For $100 the taxi driver would take me to The Twin Coves. Everyone on Eleuthera knew where the house was located. A bunch of drunks from England had just filmed a movie entitled THREE at the very place. The sex kitten, Kelly Book, and Titanic's star, Billy Zane, had tried to give the film credibility. Ah distinctly I remember, though my body hurt, but limber, Mingo, the name of the driver. The green branches of so many tropical plants slapping our window as we spiraled through the heart of darkness.

And then, we were there. One yellow outside light reflecting my dream.

Mingo helped me up the steps and into the house. I laid on the floor looking at the shadow of a ceiling fan as Mingo explained all that had happened to my redheaded wife, Chesteen, a beautiful lady and school principal.

"Well, you've got us off to a great vacation," spoke Chesteen. "I hate to think how much you'll owe for the van." She walked to a bedroom and said that it was mine. Then, she walked past me, disappearing to the other side of the large house.

My left side was beginning to increase in pain. Needles were jabbing into me. It was all I could do to breathe and not cry. I felt like Richard Burton in NIGHT OF THE IGUANA. I went to the adjoining kitchen. It was a huge old yellow tiled thing built at the end of WW2 by New York millionaires. I opened the refrigerator. There, alone, queerly, stood a quart of unopened coconut rum. The exact same brand I had battled all day and night. I had no pain pills. Mingo had not offered me any marijuana. I did the only thing an Estill Countian could.

I took the bottle.

I crawled back to my bed and unscrewed the top. Profusely, I drank. I had to fight the pain. In a while, I was back into coconut heaven. In my mind as well as outside the tallest of Palm trees swayed against an island sky. And make no mistake. The night sky of the outer islands is special.

And then, the bed collapsed. Not all of it. Just the two legs at the end where my feet where. The drop had jarred my body sending pain. I took another drink. I laid there a few minutes with my body inclined looking at the ceiling fan remembering

Martin Sheen in Apocalypse Now. Then, the ceiling fan stopped and a small electrical fire began at its center. I got to a switch and turned it off. Again, the pain continued and I had another drink. Or was it two. Maybe, three. Possibly, four. At some point as I lay silken sad, I thought I felt something lick my toe. Was I dreaming? A few minutes later, I felt the lick again. Yes, it was real. I was certain. I leaned to turn on a night lamp near the bed, again feeling sharp pain. After locating the lamp's chain, I turned to see a rat. Not just any rat. A rat as big as a groundhog. The rat was at the bottom of my bed. Quite tame. He stared at me with all the indifference in the world and wondered why I had interrupted his Kentucky toe dinner.

As dry leaves before the wild hurricane fly, I sprang from my bed. It was not the night before Christmas. Far from it. For a full minute, I was Errol Flynn in Captain Blood. Only, I was naked. My sword was a rum bottle. And All the King's men were one growling rat. For some time, I jousted, employing all my Estill County instincts. Estill County is loaded with rats. All in high offices.

Attack and defense. Man, verses beast. At long last my willpower won out and I cornered the giant in the kitchen. As Thor, I burst the bottle over the rat's head, exploding the floor in brains, blood and coconut rum. I fell to one side like Spartacus and in came Chesteen. She had no idea of the struggle or what had led up to it. "YOU'RE REALLY SETTING A FINE EXAMPLE FOR YOUR DAUGHTER!" she declared, shaking her head in disgust, turning off the light, disappearing. I struggled across the floor. The kitchen looked like the end of the third day at Gettysburg. I felt like Lee. The rum was vanquished. The word, Eleuthera, is a Greek word meaning, freedom. I didn't feel free. The ocean smell of morning was near, my comfort. I was never meant to live in Kentucky. I am one with the sea. But for all my sins I have been exiled there. The very worst of all tortures. Particularly, Estill County.

As dawn made its presence I thought of The Bataan Death March. There's nothing like being on vacation. All year long I had lied, stolen, cheated and even worked to be here.

While I nodded nearly napping, suddenly there came a tapping, as of someone gently rapping, rapping at my chamber door. Who else but this big guy named John that I met at The Sunset Inn a year ago. I'd promised, I would take him diving upon my arrival. He hadn't forgotten. He owned all the patience of a giant termite. I had absolutely no idea who the man was or what he did. Well, I did have suspicions. I figured, with all his talk of owning several homes, jet-setting around in the Caribbean and his mention of Columbia more than once, that he was in the sugar business. And not Betty White's. He had once made a manic jeep drive, cutting through the jungle showing me one of his houses. I'm sure we left a muffler and transmission somewhere in the thick. So, goes a jeep rental. But hey, who was I now, to talk of treating vehicle rentals with kindness? He also had showed me a sailboat he winched to that house. The boat supposedly hit a reef out in the ocean in front of his place. Who knew? You could see right off he had a lot of Estill County blood running in his veins. The way he treated beer with no mercy I was sure he was from Estill County, whether he knew it or not.

Chesteen directed him off in my direction. It was as though she was directing the garbage man to where the garbage was located. I was peering at a coconut tree when he entered my bedroom. "Are you ready?" he asked.

Pain dominated my left side. I felt like I'd been shot out of a cannon to a planet yet discovered. "I can't today," I responded. "I wrecked a van, went 300 feet over a cliff. My left side hurts. I can barely take the pain."

"Roll over," spoke John.

I wasn't sure why a drug lord was asking me to roll over. He proceeded to touch my side and ask me smart questions. He sounded just like some doctor. "You talk like a doctor," I said.

"I am a doctor," said John.

"A real doctor?"

"Yes. From the best I can tell, you have four broken ribs. There isn't anything I can do. If you went to a hospital, all they would do is wrap you."

"Just give me some time. We'll dive next week."

John left. I heard his rental jeep knock down a tree on the way out. At least some fresh coconuts would be on the ground. I wasn't sure if voodoo was practiced on Eleuthera. He only said he was a real doctor. Never said what kind.

A week or so must have passed. My luggage arrived. I assembled all my illegalities. Treasure was out there. So were lobsters, both out of season. I had cried my 96 tears. Each droplet, the exact same solution as The Caribbean Sea. Only more polluted. What should have happened did not and somehow, as if Lazrus,I rose from the situation with pain and bruised ribs to somehow manage to continue in life.

I found myself in conversation at the Coco de Mama's bar with a man named Jim. He was running a marine biology school. There didn't seem to be a drop of marine biology in him. He bragged about the money he was clearing on his operation. He kept trying to feel me out. As the coconut rum continued, I explained, I was a great archeologist. Kentucky's finest secret. I found lost cities as easily as you could order a happy meal at Macdonald's. After a few more rums, I elucidated, Jacques Cousteau and Mel Fisher didn't have anything on me. Or, was it Mark Spitz?

Jim asked me if I knew about skeletons. The question was going somewhere. I told him that I had dug several hundred burials. Had a degree in anthropology. Was tutored about skeletons by Lathiel Duffield at The University of Kentucky. The best biological anthropologist in America.

Jim eyeballed me right hard and asked if I knew a white man's skeleton from some other race. I told him that I was from Estill County. From the land time forgot. That evolution had been going backwards there since Adam and Eve. I explained that I knew the difference between an orangutan and a republican, which takes years of careful study. And that there was little about a skeleton which I didn't know, especially if it was the frame of some gorgeous dame. I'd been studying those skeletons a damn long time much to my travail. After hearing all that and me buying him four more coconut rums he concluded, I was an expert of some kind. He invited me to be at his marine biology school at dawn. I was told that one of Eleuthera's native bushman had found a secret cave wherein a skeleton was just inside its entrance. The Eleutherainian was afraid to go near. Jim wanted me to conduct a skeletal analysis.

When morning broke, I was at Jim's place. It was a wonderful set up, thrown together with driftwood. Something like Swiss Family Robinson and Robinson Crusoe would have imagined. Chesteen tagged along wearing a black thong bikini. Correct attire for serious anthropological studies. Our Eleutherainian appeared. Jim's wife eyed Chesteen and slammed the screen door behind us as we left.

We jeeped northward along The Queen's Highway until we finally came to a turn off near Hatchet Bay. We drove over red dirt that supposedly blew in from the Sahara. Going past The Hatchet Bay Cove we went over a hill and eventually parked in grass that was the height of a basketball goal. In Kentucky it's the only measurement we know -- that, and how far it is to the nearest bootlegger.

We whacked through the weeds with machetes. I saw Chesteen and myself as Deborah Kerr and Stewart Granger in KING SOLOMON'S MINES. You couldn't see where you were going. And only knew where you had come from by the trail you left behind. I trekked through the bush in board shorts and sandals packing a camera, frog-light, and a quart of coconut rum, standard Bahamian anthropological equipment. After much of going this way and that we arrived at the queerest of places. A naturally formed coral Stonehenge. Spiders were everywhere. Off to the left was a small overhang. The bushman pointed towards it and backed away. I leaned down and entered. Raising back up I saw a large room before me. The air was dank. In the middle of the foreboding room was a pond of water. Near my feet lay a skeleton. It was Indian. The teeth. Extreme cranial deformation. A male in his 30's. A smoker. Ate ground food. Had been strong and healthy. No trauma. An Indian, alright. An Arawak. The Arawak were the first people Columbus met when he voyaged to the New World. They were a people having originated out of the Amazon. When Columbus came to Eleuthera, it was called, Cigatoo. After he enslaved and Christianized the Arawak they soon became extinct.

There are four tides in a day. We were lucky to be at this tidal cave during low tide. It allowed us to continue our journey. As we walked through the middle of the cave in the cool water our feet often sank in the mud. In the water we saw several skeletons. I continued to stop and talk about each one to Jim and Chesteen. Some skeletons were on high areas above the water. One male had a conch which had been made into a horn beside him. After some three hundred feet or so we reached the end of the cavern. There, at the back, were three skeletons, an old woman with two young girls. There was something beguiling about them. I couldn't say what. But I felt their presence. Sometimes, I feel things. Things that are haunting and true. They had been close to each other. A grandmother and her granddaughters. I counted eighteen burials total. It was the largest group of Arawak ever discovered. Jim had a camera and was shooting the entire trip.

You don't always have to be blind stinking drunk to have a good time. But it helps. I was drunk on Arawak. I picked up the skull near the entrance and without all the scientific clay modeling, I could visualize the man's face. Very smooth features. Almost feminine. He owned a most dramatic sloping forehead. From his supraorbital margin his entire frontal eminence went straight back rounding off into something of a cone. Very extreme. Very beautiful. Such a shame that Columbus ruined everything. Flying flags at half-mast on Columbus Day should be enforced.

It was better than the front-page story once headlined in Estill County's newspaper: "MISSING LINK DISCOVERED ON BARNES MOUNTAIN!" That wasn't news. Everyone knew that missing links lived on Barnes Mountain. On Pea Ridge and Cobb Hill, too. I got a gallon of second run off rye from them every Thanksgiving. Stuff that would make you slap your grandma.

I was a child and she was a child, in this kingdom by the sea. Chesteen, she watched as I laid the skull back down. It was vexing to hold the head of a man that surely saw Columbus. I kept pondering the cave. Both sexes. All ages. Dying at the same time. Does smallpox leave a sign on bones? There were voices inside that cave. I heard them. I felt an ethereal presence. Burial caves are like that.

The next morning, Chesteen and I jeeped to the north end of Eleuthera to locate "Preacher's Cave." In 1648, Captain William Sayles and a group of Puritans set sail from Bermuda in search of religious freedom. They wrecked on the reefs and found refuge in a large blue tinted cliff where they lived and held sermons.

Leastways, that's the story. I figured if any of it was true I had a chance of finding something. As fate dictated, I discovered a large iron chest several feet deep. Nothing was in it. It was too heavy to bring back. I salvaged its odd iron and brass lock, wonderful workmanship for the period.

On our way back, we stopped at The Rainbow Inn to have a coconut rum, or was it two, maybe three and possibly four. I noted black glass bottles from the 1700's and the 1800's standing at various places throughout the bar. After hurricanes, the bottles were found in Governor's Harbour.

The next morning found me at low tide in the middle of the settlement on the Caribbean side. I was amazed to see so much black glass washed ashore. Necks to rum, wine and gin bottles. Pontiled bases indicating the 1700's to the 1800's. Pieces of early crock and transfer ware as well as iron buckles were there for the taking. I smelled a wreck. I walked out to waist deep water continuing to find Dutch and English pieces. Then I saw the most beautiful blue something. I reached down and got it-- a glass bead. It was multi-sided. Each side owned several cartouches. Egyptian. How a relic from Egypt made its way to the Harbour was a story. An Estill Countian finding it, another.

The early morning buzz is well the best. Estill Countians know this. And since that may be correct it wasn't correct the next morning. The tapping at my chamber door was a representative from Stanton Cooper, the gentleman who had rented me the Ford van. I was handed something of an itemized bill for the destruction I had wrought.

$16,543.

I looked at the bill with Estill County eyes. The way those numbers trailed off. Bogus bills are bread and butter in Estill. I had never seen so much scribbling, inserting and corrected erasing. This guy needed formal Estill County training. "Come on in," I said. "Would you like to have something to drink?" You could see the man was standing there wide-eyed and rather expectant that I was going to reach into the atmosphere and hand him around twenty grand. A rich tourist such as I had money coming out of my ears. Or so he hoped. I went into the kitchen and emptied out nearly a half quart of coconut rum over ice into two large glasses and returned with a smile. He took a sip and then another. I knew he would. If it's anything Estill Countians have an instinct about, it's a fellow con artist and drunk. Both just have a natural way of going together. I asked the man about the merits of fresh coconut water and gin, a most prescribed concoction employed by the natives. He smiled, knowing we were on the same wave length. "Look," I said, "I'm not rich. I work in a warehouse. I've been demoted all my life. Sometimes they must create new positions just so there is something lower than I already am. My father was born in a tent in a coal mining camp. He sold fruit and vegetables on the street. I was raised on whatever went rotten."

The man threw back his head and downed the whole cup. I did the same. I exited to the kitchen and emptied out the rest of the bottle. I didn't throw the bottle away. You never knew when another rat would appear. Four or two legged. Jousting with the two-legged variety is always more formidable. Fortunately, I had lucked into a universal weapon. I returned to my bill collector handing him the drink. I held up the piece of paper. Hardly a word was spelled correctly. There were three different instances where the same destroyed item was listed in different places. "You have down that I owe for a broken antennae and radio. There wasn't a radio in that van."

"Did I put that down there?"

"Right here. Six hundred and fifty-four dollars and thirty two cents."

I almost appreciated the way the man had the cents figured in on each item. It almost gave it that feel of being real. I handed the bill to the man. He took another big drink and studied it withdrawing his pencil from his shirt pocket. He began erasing several areas and re-adding. He then handed it back to me.

$4,433.22.

I liked those figures but they still needed improving. "My uncle is in the used car business," I informed. "a stalwart within our community. Occasionally, I go with him to the sales. I know what vehicles cost. And I know that that van wouldn't have even got a bid. It was nothing but scrap. It's a testament to my driving abilities that I was able to get it as far as it went."

The man finished his drink and asked for the bill. He took his pencil and marked a giant "X" through everything and wrote a number at the bottom.

$1,000.

I looked at the figure. It was round. This was more like it, an honest bunch of numbers. After all, the van had already been salvaged. God only knew about what was what regarding insurance. I never could get a straight answer. The Ford was over in the bushes. The natives had picked its skeleton down clean. "This is still a little high. But I guess fair is fair. I can't give you the thousand right now. I still have two more weeks' vacation. I don't know how my money will hold. I've got a family to worry about. They must eat. Give me your name and address. When I get back to Kentucky, I'll send you the money."

I always go to the sea. When I am not there, I am still going. I always go to the sea. If not in body, then in mind. I love her and she loves me.

THE END

ABOUT THE AUTHOR

"No Sweat" got his name when the owner of the dive shop he was working for asked him to jump in the water there at the dock where they kept their boat and kill that damn tiger shark which kept hanging around and scaring off business. After he brought in the 869-pound monster, she said, hellfire, I'm naming you, No Sweat. All summer long, he took the name to be an honor. After he got back to Kentucky, he kept on using the name. And the people of Kentucky, thought the name was perfect for him, but for altogether other reasons, none too laudable.

Born August 23, 1951, he was the first living baby of his mother; before him, she had two miscarriages. He never breathed when he was first born and the doctor pitched him in the garbage before she found out how long he could hold his breath. When he was four months old, some stranger found him jay-bird naked, crawling across the Irvine Bridge at 2:00 AM.

Earl Lowell "Robbie" / "No Sweat" Robbins, Jr, was thrown in the Irvine, Kentucky jail when he was 15 for BREACH OF PEACE. And in 1969, he graduated at the bottom of his Irvine High School class. The only thing that saved him was his wife, Chesteen. And she ain't done much of a job.

Telling lies is an art. And so, I took to writing. Any decent author is a good liar. Me having grown up in Estill County, placed me at a great advantage.

Known world-wide for his racing pigeons, No Sweat puts his family first and writing second. Pigeons come in third and after that, a bunch of stuff. BLACK BLUEGRASS is his fifth book. He's vowed, before he dies, he will have ten. As he approaches age 67, he shovels coal in a heat plant to make a living.

BOOKS BY "NO SWEAT"

1. **_THESE PRECIOUS DAYS_** --- Published 2012---Old Seventy Creek Press--- Rudy Thomas, editor.

2. **_NEFARIOUS_**---Published 2012---Itoh Press---Carol Itoh, editor.

3. **_SINGER ISLAND AND ERNEST HEMINGWAY, VOLUMES I & II_**--, - Published 2016---Old Seventy Creek Press, Rudy Thomas, editor.

4. **_LETTERS FROM A GENIUS TO AN OAF_**---Published 2017---Monday Creek Publishing---Gina Mcknight, editor.